Aubrey
and the
TERRIBLE
SPIDERS

Horatio Clare's first book for children, *Aubrey and the Terrible Yoot* (Firefly 2015) won the Branford Boase Award and was longlisted for the Carnegie Medal. The second in the series, *Aubrey and the Terrible Ladybirds* (2017) was longlisted for the UKLA book awards.

Horatio also writes award-winning adult non fiction including *Running for the Hills*, *A Single Swallow*, *Down to the Sea in Ships* and *Heavy Light*. His essays and reviews appear in the national press and his work is regularly commissioned for BBC radio.

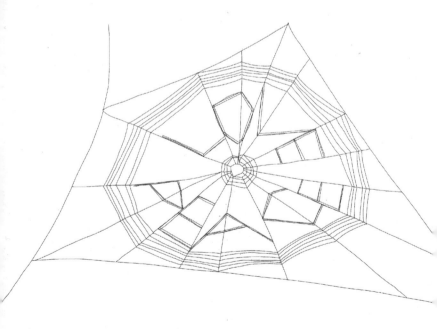

Aubrey
and the
TERRIBLE
SPIDERS

HORATIO CLARE

ILLUSTRATED BY
JANE MATTHEWS

Firefly

Published by Firefly Press
25 Gabalfa Road, Llandaff North,
Cardiff, CF14 2JJ
www.fireflypress.co.uk

A CIP catalogue record of this book
is available from the British Library.
1 3 5 7 9 8 6 4 2
Print ISBN 9781913102128
epub ISBN 9781913102135

This book has been published with the support
of the Books Council of Wales.

Design by: Becka Moor
Printed and bound by CPI Group (UK) Ltd, Croydon, CR0 4YY

FSC
www.fsc.org
MIX
Paper | Supporting
responsible forestry
FSC® C171272

Also in this series:

Aubrey and the Terrible Yoot
Aubrey and the Terrible Ladybirds

Aubrey and the Terrible Yoot won the Branford Boase
Award and was longlisted for the Carnegie Medal.

Aubrey and the Terrible Ladybirds was longlisted for
the UKLA book awards.

CHAPTER 1

You Can't Catch Chickens

Catching a chicken is much harder than catching a shark. Stick a lump of meat on a hook and throw it into some sharky water and you will have a shark in no time. Try that with chickens and they will just give you funny looks. Chickens are descended from birds called Red Jungle Fowl. That tells you something.

'If they were as big as sheep, you could tackle them!' Aubrey shouted to his mother, Suzanne, who had just tried and failed to catch one.

It was a beautiful evening in the early summer. Sunlight was still catching the leaves. Midges were dancing in clouds of dots over the beck and Aubrey was having an interesting day. He had been chased by three wasps which had seemed determined to follow him about, as if he were wearing black and eating a jam sandwich.

While he ran pell-mell through the meadow below his house shouting 'BUZZ OFF, WASPS!' and other things, and trying to swipe the insects with sticks and bracken stalks, he had not noticed a small head watching him over the wall by the lane.

The head belonged to Edie Morris. Edie was almost always up to something. Today Edie was taking a close interest in Aubrey. The two were friends in school. They had not spent that much time together, but they liked each other and they laughed at the same things. Aubrey had noticed that Edie hardly ever used more words than she needed, that she read books that made the teachers look surprised, and that you never knew what she was going to do next.

Wasps hate black and love jam. It's just

the way they are. But Aubrey was wearing
shorts and a t-shirt. As far as he knew,
wasps have no problems with these things.
But who can tell, really?

Anyway, right now, Aubrey and his mum
Suzanne were trying to catch chickens.
The woman who owned the birds, their
friend Jayne, was in Belgium, playing a
rock concert to Belgian Goths. When Jayne
asked Suzanne and Aubrey if they wouldn't
mind putting her chickens away, they said
of course they wouldn't – but that was after
watching Jayne do it. Jayne made it look
easy.

She said: 'Bedtime girls!' and opened the
coop. In the birds went.

Now Jayne was four hundred miles away
wearing black lipstick and singing about
misery to a crowd of Goths, which made
them very happy, while back in Britain
her chickens had turned into a bunch of

ferocious guerrillas. Like all guerrillas, they were using The Land to their advantage.

The Land, as everyone called it, was a lovely wild patch of nettles and briars between the playing field and the first big bend in the beck. There were all sorts of manky old buildings, weird huts, broken fences, piles of rotted garden furniture and old sheets of glass lying around on the bit Jayne owned. It was the ideal place for a chicken hunt, if you were a chicken, and the perfect place for guerrilla war, if you were a guerrilla.

'They're not faster than us ... I could definitely ... beat one in a race,' Aubrey panted. 'But they change direction really quickly!'

He almost got close enough to Pinny to touch her tail as she scooted under the coop.

'And they jump and DUCK!' cried Suzanne, lunging at a hen named Ginny.

Ginny dived sideways and evaded her.

'You're just about to get one and they do that fly-jumping thing!' Aubrey shouted, laughing as a black hen named Barbara did exactly that, flapping her wings in a wild panicky manner which looked silly until it propelled the whole chicken out of reach, like a fat bee doing a space jump.

Suddenly there was a BUZZING sound by his ear. He ducked, and a wasp shot past him.

'Wasps again!' he yelled. Seizing a whippy stick, he swished wildly at the wasp, which flew out of reach. Boy and wasp faced each other. 'Come on then!' Aubrey cried, and charged the wasp. The wasp thought better of it and flew off.

'What's got into these wasps?' he said.

'What's got into these chickens?' Suzanne asked.

She looked straight at Aubrey then, because she knew he had an unusual relationship with animals and birds. His exploits had led Suzanne to believe that her son knew how animals thought. In fact, he understood everything any creature said. You could call it a superpower, but Aubrey never did. It was just something he could do, like some people can do handstands.

'It's Barbara,' he said. 'She's telling them

to sleep out – and she's making Edgar think it's his idea.'

Edgar was the cockerel. His green and gold feathers and his scarlet wattles were magnificent.

Aubrey had been a bit wary of cockerels ever since he had been attacked by one. He was not planning to take any nonsense from Edgar.

'Get in the coop, Edgar,' he said, like he meant it.

Edgar looked completely flummoxed. Either he was faking or he was very dim.

Jayne, Aubrey remembered, murmured baby sounds and made a kind of hopping movement with her eyes. He tried it. Edgar immediately jumped into the coop.

'Got you!' Aubrey said. Edgar narrowed his eyes. Just for an instant he did not look dim at all.

Now Suzanne tried to persuade Ginny and

Pinny into the henhouse. The hens went under it, not into it.

Suzanne rolled her eyes.

'Edgar says sleep out!' Barbara clucked slyly.

'Sleep OUT!' shouted Edgar.

He looked surprised and crowed loudly to cover his confusion. 'Time to get UP!' he yelled.

He jumped out of the coop.

'Back IN!' said Aubrey.

He grabbed Edgar and stuck him back in.

'Oppression!' yelled Barbara. 'Rebel! Run! Hide!'

The chickens squawked and dashed in all directions.

'What's got into you?' Aubrey demanded of Barbara. 'Surely you need to go to bed – or the fox will get you?'

'Humans bad!' Barbara clucked. 'Chickens say NO!'

'If you think we're bad, wait until you

meet the foxes and the cats. You'll be chicken nuggets.'

'COCKERELS SAY NO!' screamed Edgar, looking incredibly proud of himself.

'We could set Lupo on them,' Aubrey said. Lupo was Aubrey's husky pup. He was a year old, and the runt of his litter, which meant he was small for a husky and full of bounce. The arrival of Lupo on Aubrey's birthday a year ago had been one of the best things that had ever happened to the little boy. Lupo had become like a brother to him. The boy and the dog loved each other, despite Lupo's bad habits. For hundreds of years huskies were bred to be fast and strong and pull sledges. Lupo's instincts meant he did not come back when you called him; he would chase sheep, cows and chickens if he got the chance. At home he was a bandit – he would raid the bins and steal food from the kitchen. He looked a bit like a guilty dingo when he was caught out doing something mischievous; Jim, Aubrey's father, had nicknamed him the Bin Dingo*. Now the Bin Dingo was tied to a post by his lead on the edge of The Land, and he was going wild with frustration at not being able to chase the chickens.

'I don't think that would be a good idea,' said Suzanne. 'He'd kill them.'

'I suppose he would,' said Aubrey.

'He definitely would. Like many children have an instinct which makes them curious about swords and guns, lots of dogs have an instinct to kill chickens. The difference is the dogs will always want to eat the chickens but children grow out of swords and guns!'

Aubrey grinned. He and his mother had a long-standing disagreement over weapons. Aubrey found toy guns and missiles fascinating. Suzanne hated them.

FOOTNOTE: Dingoes are beautiful and ancient wild dogs which live in Australia.

A crow named Corone had been watching the goings-on around the coop. Now Corone yelled, 'Chickens say NO!' in his loud kaarking voice. He flew off to find someone to tell. He met some magpies who were hanging around at the edge of the village cricket pitch looking for trouble.

Corone told them about the chickens' revolt.

The magpies told the jackdaws who lived on Mr Greenwood's farm.

The jackdaws told Mr Greenwood's sheep, his cows, his chickens, his geese, his cats, his daughter's rabbit Dennis* and his sheep dogs.

FOOTNOTE: Dennis is actually a doe called Serena.

CHAPTER 2

You Still Can't Catch Chickens (or Sheep, Pigs, Cows, Horses or Goats, for that Matter)

Meanwhile, back on the Land, the chickens were still winning.

'We can't catch them!' said Suzanne. She looked flushed and happy. Running marathons and chasing chickens seemed to light her up.

'Can I get my catapult?' Aubrey suggested, helpfully.

He had a catapult which would have knocked sense into or out of anything smaller than a whale shark. Aubrey was not really sure when his enthusiasm for weapons had begun. When he was really quite young he said to his father, Jim, 'Dad, what's the most powerful bomb in the world?'

Jim tried always to answer his son's questions honestly.

'That would be the nuclear bomb, Aubrey,' he said.

'Can I have one?'

'No.'

'Can I have a toy nuclear bomb?'

'No. In fact, they don't make toy nuclear bombs.'

'Why not?'

'Well, because the nuclear bomb is so terrible, so very powerful, that people don't like to think about them. Nuclear bombs could destroy the entire world. So we hope and pray no one ever fires one, and we definitely don't make toys out of them.'

Aubrey thought about this. As time went by his interest in weapons grew and he noticed many of his friends thought the same way. He saw them in games, on screens and in films, and they heard about them from other children, especially older children. By the time of our story, Aubrey and his friends, like many other children, could tell you all about grenades, machine-guns, rifles and rockets. His parents would not let him have any of them, but he had acquired two toy guns which fired foam darts, a toy revolver which didn't do anything but did look cool, several NERF guns, a toy sub-machine gun which no longer made a crackling sound and a catapult. He did not want to hurt anything but he did spend quite a lot of time thinking about shooting imaginary baddies with imaginary guns. Now he was imagining using his catapult on these rebellious chickens.

Suzanne shook her head.

'They're just like wild kids,' she said. 'Let's bribe them.'

Aubrey loaded a scoop with corn and filled the chickens' trough.

'Come on, ladies! Come on, Edgar!' Suzanne called. 'Jump up!'

Aubrey listened to the birds' reactions.

'Cornfood?' clucked Hegarty.

'Bribe!' shouted Barbara. 'Rebel! Sleepout! No bribes!'

'FOOD-A-FOODLE-FOOD!' yelled Edgar. He jumped in and began stuffing himself, gleefully, as if he had never tried corn before. His wattles wibbled with delight.

Hegarty, Ginny and Pinny seemed to sigh before they followed him in.

Now Barbara faced Suzanne and Aubrey.

Barbara looked as ready for a fight as it is possible for a big black chicken to look.

'Get her!' cried Suzanne.

She and Aubrey moved in fast.

Barbara dashed between them.

'Right. Barbara can take her chance with the foxes,' Suzanne decided.

She winked at Aubrey. He grinned like a wolf: an alarming sight if you are a chicken. Not for nothing was his wild name Aubrey Rambunctious Wolf. He imagined a steaming chicken fresh out of the oven, bolstered by roast potatoes and sloppy with gravy. His mouth watered.

Barbara clucked in alarm, ran between them again and jumped for the coop.

Suzanne dashed in and shut the door.

'Got her!' she laughed. 'Phiieew!'

'Yes, Mum! High five!'

'Never again,' muttered Barbara. Aubrey could hear her quite clearly through the door.

CHAPTER 3

News of the News Reaches the News

Now the strange days began.

Mr Greenwood went to move some sheep to the meadow below Aubrey's house. The sheep sat down and refused to budge.

Mr Greenwood's sheep dog, Fly, who could trick sheep into doing anything normally, was suddenly useless. She gambolled about with the butterflies. The sheep ignored her.

When Mr Greenwood tried to get his cows

out of their barn, they mooed at him and wagged their heavy heads. When he tried to shoo them, they looked at him as if to say, 'Really? You think?'

Mr Greenwood became so hot and confused he had to lie down.

Jackdaws, magpies and crows spread news of the Great Rebellion across the country. Animals everywhere joined in.

Ducks ducked.

Chickens dodged.

Horses ambled off.

Sheep shook their heads.

Pig farmers were knocked off their feet.

Ninety-two parrots, 38 egrets, 7 mynah birds, 23 ibis, 17 bulbuls and 12 Narina trogons escaped from London Zoo. No one could work out how they had done it.

Next, news of the news reached the News. With the animals refusing to be bossed around it became impossible to get those that were supposed to be eaten into trailers and lorries. Shops and butchers ran out of bacon, ham, chicken, turkey, guinea fowl, steak, sausages and lamb.

By the end of the third day no mince, no burgers, chops, drumsticks or meat of any kind was available anywhere in the country. People tried to order meat online. You can imagine how well that went: expensive chaos.

Unless you had meat in your freezer, you ate vegetables or fish. With many people suddenly wanting fish, the price of fish rocketed. Soon there were hardly any fish products in the shops: some people went straight to the ports and bought fish from fishermen, who couldn't believe their luck. There was not even close to enough to go around, though.

Bye-bye, fish fingers.
Farewell, smoked salmon.

So long, haddock fillets.
Laters, cod in parsley sauce.

By the fourth evening, only vegetables
and fruit remained.

FOOTNOTE: You could still get
crabsticks because one thing crabsticks
do not contain is crab. True! Check, if
you don't believe me.

FOOTNOTE TO FOOTNOTE: I
could be wrong about this. I have only
actually read two crabstick packets.
Both contained crabsticks. Neither
contained crab: these are crabs'
favourite kind.

CHAPTER 4

Life and Wasps
(or Be Careful What You
Wish For)

Like everyone else, Aubrey and his family followed the news of the Great Animal Rebellion with amazement. Lupo the husky pup might have joined the rebellion, too, but it was hard to tell. He never did what you told him to anyway. He wagged his tail, looked at you with love and carried on being a lawless bandit bin dingo. Jim and Suzanne laughed at him but they muttered to each other and, knowing how close Aubrey was to animals, kept a worried eye on their son.

'You won't disappear on one of your adventures, will you?' they begged him.

Aubrey said he was not looking for any

adventures. That was true. He did not say he was really hoping an adventure would find him. When it did (adventures always know where to look) it found him at school.

Class Two was doing maths. Miss Hannah was explaining long multiplication. Aubrey was concentrating. The scent of summer came in through the open windows.

Out of the corner of his eye Aubrey was aware of an insect flying towards him. Next, he felt the lightest brush on his arm. He heard a small voice say, 'Sorry. Orders.'

He looked down. A wasp had landed on him. Before he could swipe it off or twitch his arm away, the wasp curled its bottom and stung him.

'OW!' he shouted, jumping up.

'What is it, Aubrey?' cried Miss Hannah.

'OW!' he shouted again. 'Wasp sting! OWWW!'

It really hurt. His eyes filled with tears.
Other children jumped up looking panicked,
although the wasp had already flown out of
the window.

One child was furious. It was Jolyon, a big boy who always sat at the back.

'Aubrey loves animals, but they don't love him!' Jolyon shouted. He was furious on behalf of his friend. The other children understood why: everyone knew Aubrey loved animals – how dare one of them hurt him?

'I hate wasps!' cried Gareth.

'I hate bees!' shouted Ella. 'And spiders are disgusting!'

'Insects are disgusting,' cried Little Steven.

Big Steven agreed. 'Insects and fish,' he said. 'Yuk.'

Miss Hannah took control.

'Jolyon, don't be cross. Let us be cool, please. Quiet down, everyone. Aubrey, go and ask Mrs Grayson for vinegar. Put some on the sting. Go!'

Aubrey went. Mrs Grayson was in charge of school dinners. She was very kind and efficient. In no time the acid in the vinegar neutralised the wasp venom and it soon stopped hurting much.

After the sting, despite the perfect summer afternoon, Aubrey did not feel like playing outside so he went to the library and read a book called *Great Battles in History*. He was not alone among the shelves of books. The other child there was Edie Morris. Edie was so good at maths that the teachers had to set her special work to stop her becoming bored. Aubrey glanced at the book she was working on. It was full of algebra and strange symbols, like an alien language.

'What are you reading, Edie?'

Edie looked at him. Aubrey had the sense of being closely studied by enormous bright eyes.

'It looks like Japanese Hungarian.'

Edie laughed.

'It's called *Inorganic Phosphors: Properties of Lasers*,' she said. 'It's really interesting.'

'Wow,' said Aubrey. 'How come you are so good at maths and science? And English?'

'I'm just interested in them, like you're interested in stories and battles and animals. Your stories are the best. And you're really good at history.'

'Have you seen this Great Animal Rebellion thing?'

Edie's eyes flashed behind her glasses.

'Yes, I have. It's brilliant. I don't eat animals anyway. I prefer them to people. People have messed up the world and they want children and animals to make the best of it. I'm so glad the animals are rebelling.'

'I think me and Mum started it by mistake when we were trying to herd a chicken called Barbara.'

Edie laughed. 'That sounds like you! Changing the world...'

'If only we could!' said Aubrey.'

'We can! Children can change the world,' Edie said, fiercely. And then she said, 'I'm really sorry about your sting.'

'Just a sting,' said Aubrey, but he kept

thinking about it, and the wasps chasing him yesterday. Why had they suddenly got it in for him? He never hurt them. Aubrey remembered the small voice. He was certain the wasp had apologised before it stung him. 'Orders,' it had said. But who could have ordered it to sting him – and why?

Lying in bed later, listening to Jim's murmurs as he read to Suzanne, and watching the summer evening turning into a deep sea of sky through his window, Aubrey's thoughts were disturbed by a small and beautiful voice like the chiming of bells.

'Perfect evening, isn't it?' said the voice.

Aubrey sat up quickly.

The owner of the voice had eight hairy legs, eight eyes and two large jaws. She was only three centimetres long, from the tips of her front legs to the tips of her back legs, but that still looked like an awful lot of house spider when she turned up on your pillow.

'Ariadne!'

'Hello!'

Spider and boy were best friends. They had shared great adventures. Ariadne had a lovely, kind character. You could not tell this by looking at her. The only time Suzanne had ever seen her, when Ariadne had been trapped in the bath, Suzanne screamed and asked Aubrey to move her.

The one occasion when Jim had come across her, while he was looking for a book in the attic, he had squealed and walked away slowly, backwards. (This is how you deal with properly dangerous animals, like cobras and hippos.) Jim had ducked out of the room and slammed the door.

Aubrey told Ariadne about his problems with wasps.

'Who on earth would order a wasp to sting me?' he asked her.

'Not an animal,' Ariadne said, thought-fully. 'Ordering someone to hurt someone else is not our way. It sounds devious. We hurt to defend ourselves or our territory, or to eat. If someone ordered you to be stung for another reason, you're looking for a human.'

'But – but that would mean I'm not the only one who talks to animals!'

'Um,' said Ariadne.

'WHAT?' Aubrey yelled. 'There's someone else! Who?'

'Um, there are millions of you. Have you

never been to Kazakhstan? Uzbekistan? Turkmenistan?'

'No,' Aubrey said, 'I haven't.'

'Have you heard of the Mongols? The Anatolians? The Pashtuns? The Uighurs? The Turkomens? The Maasai? The Siberians? The Berbers? The Welsh?'

'Some of them, yes.'

'Well,' Ariadne said, thoughtfully, 'many of the world's peoples can speak to animals and birds in their own tongue. All over the planet there are people who talk to animals, birds, insects and fish.'

'FISH! Who talks to fish?'

'Fisherfolk do,' Ariadne said, solemnly. 'And everyone with a fish tank. Humans talk to their animals.'

'OK,' Aubrey nodded. 'But someone else around here also understands what animals say.'

'Um,' said Ariadne.

Aubrey looked hard at the spider. She

blinked five of her eyes. He knew he was right. Somewhere nearby he had an enemy, and that enemy had the same power he did – maybe much more power. Aubrey felt cold fear. He swallowed and hid it. By deciding to be brave he instantly felt braver. Interesting, he thought, and saved that thought for later.

'What's his name? Where is he?'

'I don't know,' Ariadne said, but then she whispered. 'They say he's got Terrible Spiders. He's making thousands of them. Millions. He's going to conquer the world with them – they're robots or drones or something. Don't say I told you. Forget it. They call him Big B. Forget that too.'

'Ariadne,' Aubrey said, after a pause, 'Please tell me everything you know about this person and these spiders. Where does Big B live? Who told you about all this?'

'Silvio mentioned it. But lots of creatures are talking about it. I've never heard of anyone who knows who he is or where he lives. It's just rumours. B's supposed to be about your age and he can talk to animals too.'

'Who is Silvio?'

'Silvio is a silverfish who...' Ariadne stopped and shifted slightly '...visits your kitchen.'

'You mean he lives there?'

'Yes.'

'Just say it then!'

'Some people don't like to be thought of as having kitchens silverfish live in.'

'Who?'

'Well, everyone who isn't you, really, Aubrey.'

'Never mind them. We need to find Big B and fight him – or them. And these spiders.'

'Do we?'

'Don't we? If we know there's a kid who can talk to animals and he's got Terrible

Spiders and he wants to conquer the world, don't we have to do something?'

Ariadne thought for a moment. 'We could ignore it,' she said.

Aubrey looked at her as though she was as wild as a wingnut.

'We really can't!'

'Why not? Humans are brilliant at ignoring things,' Ariadne said, coolly. 'Plastic in the sea. Ice caps melting. Species dying out. Lots of humans basically ignore all that.'

The boy was not sure what to say. He looked out of the window. There was a jet plane high up, crossing the blue. It was beautiful, but he could see the trail like a straight white cut, a long scar in the atmosphere behind the plane.

'Where would we start?' Ariadne asked, as if she could not help being curious.

Aubrey thought. 'If he told that wasp

to sting me then we should start with the wasp. Or the silverfish. Can I meet Silvio?'

Aubrey carried Ariadne downstairs. Jim was in the kitchen making Suzanne a cup of tea. When he saw his son carrying an enormous house spider in his palm, he went pale and he squealed.

'EEK!' he cried. 'Throw it outside!'

'This is Ariadne, Dad. She's a friend.'

'Suzanne!' Jim yelled. 'Tell Aubrey – he's got a giant tarantella! I mean tarantula. Help!'

In the living room Suzanne laughed.

'Aubrey?' she called.

Aubrey called back. 'It's fine!'

'Danger!' yelled Jim. 'Mercy!' He dashed out of the room and slammed the door.

'I really like your parents,' Ariadne said. 'Most humans make me nervous but they never do.'

'Where's Silvio?'

'He normally hangs around near the vegetable bowl. Just move that – ah! Hello, Silvio.'

The silverfish was a tiny creature like a sharpened woodlouse with two feelers, only much faster.

'Dudes,' he said.

'This is Aubrey,' Ariadne said. 'Aubrey, Silvio.'

'I know,' said Silvio. 'Howdy.'

'I think I've seen you around, too. How's it going?'

'Knackered! I was up late. Film club with your dad. We're so into spy movies.'

'You and Dad have a film club?'

'Kinda. I go up the back of the sofa and watch over his shoulder. You learn so much!'

'Like what?' Aubrey asked, grinning.

'Everything!' Silvio cried. 'I know how to hot-wire a car, how to fly a plane, how to knock someone out, how to pick a lock,

how to avoid cameras, how to break into an
embassy, how to break out of an embassy...'
Silvio was wiggling and running in circles
in short bursts, raising his front legs and
waving them. 'I know how to win a car
chase, how to win a gun fight, how to track
down suspects, how to hack computers. I
even know how to bring down a helicopter
with a peanut!'

'Which film is that in?' Aubrey asked.

'It's not. I just thought of a way.'

'That is impressive,' said Ariadne.

Aubrey agreed. 'You sound like an incredibly useful guy to know,' he said. 'An incredibly useful silverfish, I mean.'

'I think I am,' Silvio said, earnestly. 'I really think I am.'

'What do you know about Big B and the Terrible Spiders?' Aubrey asked.

'Not much.'

'But Silvio, you told me Big B was making Terrible Spiders and they were going to take over the world!' Ariadne said. 'Remember? You said Big B could talk with us?'

'OH! Hoppy the squirrel heard a sparrow say that a blue tit had told her that a crow said he saw Big B talking to a wasp and the wasp was talking back, so they must have understood each other.'

'What were they saying?'

'Hoppy said the sparrow said the blue tit said the crow didn't say.'

'I think I know,' Aubrey muttered. 'I was chased by wasps the other day and another one stung me in school. It had been ordered to do it.'

'Find that wasp, you find Big B,' said Silvio. 'Your pool of suspects is all wasps, but you can narrow it down to all the wasps around where you were stung, and the ones that chased you. Say there's a hundred nests within flying distance of the school, and each nest holds about 4000 wasps, you're looking for one in 400,000. Unless...'

'Unless what?'

'The wasp that stung you and the ones that chased you were just obeying orders!' Silvio said, laughing.

'Well, at least one wasp knows who this Big B is and where we find him,' said Aubrey.

'So we're still looking for just one wasp?' Ariadne demanded. She suddenly nipped down the back of the fridge and reappeared with a tiny insect, which she ate.

'What was that?' Aubrey asked.

'Nothing,' Ariadne said, chewing and swallowing.

'You could try setting traps around the school!' Silvio exclaimed.

'I thought I might web the window of Aubrey's classroom,' Ariadne told Silvio. 'Tomorrow.'

'Oh, you did?' Aubrey cried. He was delighted. 'So you are going to help?'

'Mm. Haven't decided,' Ariadne said. 'Quite fancy a wasp for lunch though.'

'Good thinking,' said Silvio. 'But you need another line of investigation in case it doesn't work. We should ask wasps if they have heard of any of their lot working with Big B. Even a rumour. Someone is sure to have heard something.'

'I don't know any wasps,' said Aubrey.

'I've met one or two,' Ariadne put in, 'but I paralysed them and sucked their innards out before we got to know each other.'

'There's a nest at the end of the Ferrabys' garden,' Silvio said. 'You could start there.'

'What happens if they decide to attack me?' Aubrey said. 'They don't like people going near their nests, do they?'

'Fill the bath to the top with water before you go,' Silvio advised him. 'If they come for you, jump in, go right under and breathe through a straw. You'll need a straw.'

'Right,' said Aubrey. He felt uncertain.

'Or you could leg it down to the beck and jump in that. You'll still need a straw.'

'Right.'

'And don't wear black. They hate it. White's good. And remember if one stings you, it sends out a signal to the others to sting you in the same place. So – run!'

'Right...'

'And – maybe you should take some insurance?' Silvio said. 'That's what I would do. A rolled-up magazine under your shirt?'

'Wouldn't taking a weapon make it more likely I'd have to use it?' Aubrey asked the tiny insect.

'Well, you know what they say about polar bears and rifles,' Silvio replied.

'What do they say about polar bears and rifles?'

'No one wants to hurt a polar bear, and no one wants to carry a rifle. But if you're in a situation with a polar bear when you wish you had a rifle, you're toast,' said the silverfish.

'Oh-kay,' Aubrey said.

'I love toast!' announced Silvio. 'When you make some in the morning, can you be sure to leave the crumbs lying about?'

'No problem at all,' said Aubrey.

CHAPTER 5

Stung Again

The next day was Saturday. Jim and Suzanne noticed Aubrey had decided to dress in his PE kit, but they did not say anything. They grinned at each other and waited to see what he was up to.

Aubrey was feeling rather scared. It is one thing to imagine going into battle with imaginary baddies who cannot actually hurt you. It is quite another thing to set out to question a swarm of crazed wasps. With a handful of straws in his pocket and the magazine stuffed down the back of his shorts, Aubrey set out for the Ferrabys' garden.

It was much neater than his. Suzanne didn't have time for gardening and Jim said wild gardens were better for nature, because they attract insects and birds.

After fighting his way through various bushes, plants and thickets, Aubrey dropped over the fence and found himself standing among the Ferrabys' neat paths and flower beds.

Mrs Ferraby agreed with Jim up to a point; the very top of her garden was a magical tangle of wild roses and honeysuckle, and here, in an old pile of logs and sticks, was the wasp nest.

Aubrey watched for a while as insects flew in and out of the woodpile. Ever since he was very small, when Jim had first shown him how to spot a wasps' nest (you look for a little cloud of big insects flying around a particular spot) the boy had stayed well clear of them.

'If you get within about three metres, that's the danger zone,' his father had told him.

'You don't get any warning; the guards will sting you straight away, to protect their nest, and if you don't get away quickly lots more wasps will come after you.'

Now Aubrey moved slowly, carefully, closer. He could see that there were three

 wasps who were not
coming and going like
the others but flying in
wonky loops around the
area of the nest.

He crept close enough to overhear them.

'I'm as bored as a rotten apple,' said one.

'I'm as bored as a dead sheep,' said
another.

'You two are always bored. Be alert!' said
the third.

'Your nest needs lerts,' chorused the other
two together.

The wasps spoke in pinched, buzzy voices,
as though they were holding their noses.

'I wish I could fight something,' said the
first wasp.

'Nothing ever happens when I'm on
duty,' the second replied. 'I haven't stung
anything for days.'

'I stung that dog...' the first began.

The other two immediately started shouting.

'That was ages ago!'

'That was last year!'

'You were still a grub. It never happened.'

'You haven't even got a sting!'

'I'll sting you now in a minute!' the first wasp screamed, at the top of his small voice.

'It's my turn for break,' the second wasp announced. 'I'm gonna get me some rotten apple. Might sting a few cats on the way back.'

'You'd never dare sting a cat, butty,' snapped the third. 'You'd never dare sting anything bigger than a caterpillar.'

'I would! I stung that badger.'

'We all stung that badger!' shouted the other two.

'I'll sting the blimmin' pair of you,' the second said, and flew off.

One guard less, Aubrey thought. He quite liked the sound of these wasps. They were slightly scary but he recognised their longing for excitement. All children know that feeling. Aubrey sidled closer to the wasps now, taking advantage of the reduction of the size of their force. He knew that a skilful solider takes advantage of every opportunity.

'Hey, there's someone coming!' cried one of the guards.

'Is he over the line? Oooh! He's not over the line. Can we sting him anyway? Come on, boys! Let's sting 'im!'

'Orders say we stay by the nest unless something crosses the line,' said the third wasp. 'Then we attack. And I am female. You KNOW that.'

'But he's so close! Let's attack. Come on –

we can always say we thought he was over the line. Please please please! Come ON!'

'No. Stick to orders.'

'Pretty please! Stuff the orders! I'm going to sting him now in a minute.'

'Stay where you are. That's an ORDER.'

'I don't take orders from you, mate.'

'Excuse me? I'm Guard Captain. You do take orders from me or I sting you, mate.'

Both wasps were now so agitated they were flying in furious circles around each other and shouting.

'Come on then! Come on – sting me!'

'Say that again and I will!'

'Yaaa, you don't dare; you're only good for stinging dopey Labradors. There's a human right there and you don't even want to sting him! What's the point of being on guard if you don't sting him? What's the point of being a wasp?'

'The point of being a wasp...' the Guard Captain began.

'Excuse me,' Aubrey said. 'Please don't sting me. It's just that I'm looking for a wasp and I wondered if you could help?'

There was a long pause.

'He's talking to you,' said the wasp who wanted to sting. 'Bet he's trying to trick you. Sting him!'

'I'm really not trying to trick you,' Aubrey said. 'There's someone I'm trying to find. And I think a wasp knows who it is.'

The third wasp now returned. None of the wasps looked impressed.

The little boy pressed on bravely.

'I am trying to find out who Big B is? I want to meet him.'

The first wasp went ballistic.

'Whatseeonaboutthen? Flippingsting'im!'

'Stop shouting or I will sting you. This

could be serious,' said the Guard Captain, calmly, with authority.

'It *is* serious,' Aubrey cried. 'I have to find this wasp who stung me because someone saw it talking to Big B. There are rumours that Big B might be doing something terrible. I need to find the wasp to find Big B.'

As he was talking Aubrey had shuffled a tiny bit closer to the wasps' nest without realising it.

Now the second wasp went ballistic. 'REALLY?' he shouted at the Guard Captain. 'Look where he is! I am going to sting him now!'

'He's over the liiinnne!' The other shouted, joyfully. 'I'm going innnnnnn!'

'WAIT!'

The Guard Captain still hadn't raised her voice but she spoke with huge authority.

'It's not a wasp you want,' she said to

Aubrey. 'Big B gave the orders to a hornet who gave them to the wasps. Find the hornet. And you are over the line. So *run*.'

Aubrey took half a breath and ran. He forgot all about drawing the magazine and fighting, which was lucky. No one can fight a whole nest of wasps with a rolled-up magazine; even three is a lot if they all attack at once.

Luckily, only two came after him. As he was diving over the fence back into his garden the first wasp got him twice on his left calf and the second wasp got him once on his right buttock.

'Ow! Ow!' he yelled. 'Ow!!'

'Got you, you crazy giant!' shouted one wasp.

'Got you twice, you big space invader!' shouted the other.

The Guard Captain tried not to laugh. 'Wait until he meets a hornet,' she said.

'Neither of them is going to have any idea what the other one is on about.'

'You lied about the hornet?' asked the first wasp.

'Misdirection,' said the Guard Captain. 'It's called misdirection.'

'Hornets eat us, and humans splat us. They should get on well,' observed the first wasp.

'Eunice?' said Mr Ferraby, who had seen the whole thing.

'Yes, dear?' Mrs Ferraby called back.

'Guess what?' said Mr Ferraby. 'I think there might be something going on next door.'

'Is it Aubrey?'

'Yes, dear.'

'Oh, good! What is he up to this time?'

'He seems to be taking up beekeeping.'

'Oh, wonderful!'

'But with wasps.'

'Crikey!' said Mrs Ferraby. 'Whatever

next? I know he likes action but that's upping the game, isn't it?'

'He often does, dear! I should keep watch, shouldn't I?'

Mr Ferraby was a huge fan of Aubrey's despite what had happened to his beloved car during the boy's first adventure.

'You bet you should,' Mrs Ferraby said. 'And tell me all about it.'

CHAPTER 6

Some Notes on the Historical Role of Hornets

In the bathroom Aubrey rubbed calamine lotion into his stings. (His childhood had had quite a few stings in it, so he knew what to do.) Ariadne was standing on the edge of the bath, shaking her head at how dangerous it was. Baths are such fun to get into and so hard to get out of, she was thinking. They really ought to have spider steps built into them.

'Where do I find this hornet, Ariadne?'

Ariadne was feeling a bit dreamy. The smooth sides of the bath made her long to slide into it.

'Just put the word out,' she said. 'The hornet will find you. They are incredibly clever.'

'How clever?'

'Clever enough to beat the Spanish Armada,' said Silvio. Silvio had come up the pipe through the floor from the kitchen.

'What?'

'You have heard of Elizabeth the First?' Silvio demanded.

'Of course,' said Aubrey, 'and Captain Sir Francis Drake, who beat the Spanish Armada.'

'Mmm. Yes – and at the same time, and in a very real sense – no,' Silvio said. 'In fact, Elizabeth had a spy master called Walsingham: he helped to keep her in power. But guess where he got his information from?'

'Don't tell me...'

'That's right! His chief adviser was a hornet called Mikhail.'

'I don't believe you.'

The little silverfish zipped up the basin pipe, climbed the outside of the basin and stood, waving his feelers, at Aubrey's eye-level.

'Believe what you like! Mikhail the Hornet gave Walsingham an accurate weather forecast. Walsingham gave it to Francis Drake and that's how Drake knew how to beat the Armada. But he wouldn't have won the battle if Mikhail hadn't told

him to send in the fireships when the
Armada was anchored. Many hornets are
geniuses of naval tactics. In the future
they will command star fleets. Darth
Vader would easily have won *Star Wars*
if George Lucas knew anything about
hornets. All Lord Vader needed was one
like Mikhail to look after him. But people
don't know anything really, do they?
Not about insects in history. The Duke
of Wellington's best friend was a hornet
called Liliana. She told him how to win
the battle of Waterloo.'

'Stop it!'

'It's Historical Fact! How do you
think Horatio Nelson won the battle of
Trafalgar?'

'Let me guess, he had a hornet named...'

'Did someone say 'Istorical Fact?' cried
a small voice. A small insect, known in
Rushing Wood as the Historian Ladybird,
perched on the bathroom window ledge.
Aubrey had met him in his previous
adventures.

'Hello!' cried Aubrey. 'Can you tell...'

'Yes, I can,' said the Ladybird. 'I 'appened to be just outside; I 'eard everything. The harmada 'ornet is true and the Waterloo 'ornet is true but there were no 'ornets involved in Trafalgar. But they did train Nelson when he was in Italy. Of course, Nelson's flagship, *The Victory* had many insects aboard, some of whom were highly influential. He relied on one or two in the plannin' phase of a battle, always, and Trafalgar was no exception.'

'That was a silverfish!' yelled Silvio, and did a small dance.

'Actually it was a weevil,' said the ladybird. 'And its advice was wrong. But Nelson wasn't in the habit of blindly following the advice of weevils, so he did his own thing and won the battle.'

'That must have been such an amazing battle!' said Aubrey. 'The canons, the muskets, the galleons – awesome.'

'Hawesome it was,' said the Historian Ladybird, 'but not in a good way. Naval warfare was 'orrendous. The ships were made of wood, so they didn't really sink. To win you basically 'ad to bleed the enemy ship to death. So you shot down its masts or shot off its rudder so it couldn't get away, and then you raked the men on the decks with canon fire and grape shot, which was bits of sharp metal. There was so much blood they used buckets of sand to soak it up, otherwise everyone would slip over. All you could hear was men screaming and crying out and the canons blasting. They didn't have much in the way of medicine either – can you imagine someone sawing off your leg while you watched? 'Istory teaches us that war is hell. And yet we still send brave young men and women to learn the lesson again. And we always tell them it's the right thing to do.'

'And is it the right thing to do?' Aubrey asked.

''Istorically speaking, it can be. If some conquering monster attacks you, and you 'aven't got a choice,' said the Historian Ladybird. 'But make no mistake about it, war is the curse of your species. If you ask people who've been in one, they'll tell you that starting a war is never right and stopping one is never wrong. Right, I'd best be off. 'Istory never stops for long! I'll put the word out about the 'ornet. It's no trouble; don't thank me.'

'Thank you!' chorused Aubrey, Ariadne and Silvio. And the Historian Ladybird was gone.

'Well, that was easy,' Aubrey said. 'My stings feel better.' 'So what about these Terrible Spiders, Ariadne? What's so special about them?'

'Tarantella,' Ariadne said. 'It's a dance.'

'Tarantella?'

'Whee-Hee!' she cried, suddenly. She jumped off the rim and slid down the long white slope into the bath.

'Weee-HEEE!' she cried again. 'I love baths!'

Aubrey laughed. 'Do you want another go?'

He lifted her up. Ariadne wanted three more goes. The spider jumped and giggled and the little boy helped her out each time.

'Yup. Tarantulas might bite you, if you're mean to them, but these tarantellas are much more serious. I heard a rumour that if they bite, you dance.'

'Is that bad?'

'I guess it depends how long you dance for,' Ariadne said. She jumped off the rim one last time and slid all the way to the bottom. She sat in the white bowl of the bath and looked up at her friend. 'I guess it depends if you can stop,' she said.

CHAPTER 7

Fighting a Hornet (by Mistake)

Villi was a hornet. When people saw Villi coming they tended to freeze and point at her in her gorgeous red and gold stripes, either in delight or in fear.

Why, you might ask, do some people fear an insect that is not even a third as long as a mobile phone? Aubrey once asked his father the same question: 'Dad, why are people scared of hornets? Aren't they just big wasps?'

'Well,' Jim said, I know a story about a man who survived a terrible battle, one of the fiercest in history, called D-Day.'

'D-Day!' Aubrey cried. 'World War Two!'

'Exactly,' said Jim. 'The Allies – the British, the Americans, the Canadians – landed in Normandy, to begin taking Europe back from the Nazis.'

'Amphibious tanks!' Aubrey said. 'Naval gunfire!'

'Exactly,' said Jim, again. 'Incredibly brave men and a horrific slaughter. Over four thousand were killed landing on those beaches. And one man, the solider in this story about hornets, survived the terrible battle on the first day. Unfortunately, he pitched his tent too close to a hornets' nest. This woke them up, and the hornets attacked, to defend their home, and a few of them stung the man, some of them twice. Having survived all those shells and bullets, he died. But here's the strange thing. The stings of the European Hornet are really not that strong. That soldier must have had an allergic reaction. However, that part of the story was lost. You just hear, hornets sting soldier, he dies; you can see how that would affect the reputation of hornets! These days we would give him an injection and he would be fine. So people are scared of them because they look scary, and their stings are more powerful than wasps'. But they are not aggressive. If you leave them alone, they will leave you alone. Just make sure you stay away from their nests.'

Now, Villi happened to be visiting the little

town near Woodside Terrace where our heroes live.

Aubrey and Villi met by chance, near the station. The encounter went wrong pretty quickly. Aubrey spotted Villi flying towards the park and cried, 'Hey! Excuse me!'

Hornets have plenty of experience of sudden interest from humans. Often it comes with a swat, a slap or a splat. Hearing a human crying out, and seeing him coming at her, Villi assumed Aubrey meant to do her harm.

Villi turned, curled her bottom forward slightly in a menacing fashion, and aimed at him. As far as she knew she was already under attack.

FOOTNOTE: All sorts of terrible fights and wars begin with rumour, mischief or misunderstanding. In 1925 a Greek soldier chasing a runaway dog was shot at by Bulgarian soldiers, which made the Greeks so angry they attacked Bulgaria. (The misunderstanding in this case was the dog's, which thought it was just having a laugh, rather than starting a war.)

'Hello!' Aubrey cried, in an excited way, 'Hey! Wait!'

But Villi flew towards him, rapidly speeding up, with her bottom curled forward. Aubrey was in no doubt that she meant to sting him.

Aubrey did not wait to be stung. He shouted, 'Holy Peter!' and lashed out in terrified self-defence. He was aware of Silvio diving off to his right.

Unfortunately for the hornet, but very luckily for Aubrey, Suzanne and Jim had sent him to Ninja Tots when he was barely old enough to hold up a tackle bag, though not too small to whack one.

He hit out with a straight right, bopping the hornet flush on the nose, and a swift left, as he had been taught, which caught Villi with a hefty blow. Villi rolled and skewed sideways, but she kept coming. Her sting flashed out; by a miracle (a miracle is about two centimetres in length) the sting missed him.

'YEEK!' yelled Aubrey.

He launched a side-sweeping kick with his left leg. Villi dodged him, rocketed sideways in mid-air and crashed into the flower tub in front of the station.

'Yes!' screamed Silvio. 'Quick! Finish it off!'

Boy looked at silverfish. Both were panting.

'You must be crazy!' Aubrey gasped. 'I don't go around killing insects. Never!'

'It's a killer!' Silvio screamed again. 'Kill it before it stings us!'

Aubrey thought fast. When he was small his parents had asked him what he wanted to do when he grew up. They were reading him lots of stories of Welsh, Irish and Greek myths at the time (Suzanne was doing a degree in Classics with the Open University) and this must have influenced his first choice of career.

'What are you going to be when you grow up, Aubrey?' Jim asked.

Aubrey had paid great attention to the stories he was told. He had noticed that his favourite stories often involved the same kinds of people.

'I'm going to be a warrior,' he announced.

'Oh!' said Jim. His face changed from happy and playful to blank and worried.

'Now, Aubrey,' Suzanne said. 'You will be a wonderful warrior, but we will only support you on one condition. There is something you must understand if you are going to be a warrior.'

'What?' Aubrey asked.

'You must be a warrior for peace,' Suzanne said.

'Yes!' Jim cried. 'Any idiot can fight in other people's wars. What the world needs are great warriors who will fight to end war, end battles, and bring peace.'

'Oh-kay,' Aubrey agreed, thoughtfully.

Now Aubrey was a long way from grown up and something inside him had never stopped being a warrior in training.

'Stomp it!' howled Silvio.

Aubrey advanced on the stunned insect.

'Last chance, hornet,' he said. 'Tell me where Big B is.'

'We're not going to ask you twice,' Silvio put in. Silvio was riding on Aubrey's shoulder now and looking mighty brave and fierce, for a silverfish. 'Talk fast, stripy!'

As you can imagine, Villi was dazed and cross. She made an angry buzzing, which sounded scary enough, although really it was all she could do.

Aubrey bent down and looked at her. This was no longer an enemy with the power to hurt him. This was a befuddled insect;

big for an insect but tiny compared to a human. 'How many spiders,' Ariadne had once asked him, 'do humans splat every day? Hundreds and hundreds every minute, thousands a day, millions a week. Because you're scared of us? How wrong it that!'

And Aubrey agreed with her. He thought it was wrong to kill insects just because you are scared of them.

The insect on his shoulder disagreed with him. 'Whack it!' shouted Silvio. 'Hornets are evil!'

'Because they might eat you?'

'Because they might eat me!' Silvio agreed.

'Have you ever heard of a hornet eating a silverfish?'

'No!'

Aubrey sat down on the edge of the flower tub. Villi stopped buzzing. She was all out of fight. She rearranged her wings and gathered her breath*.

'Do you think you might be watching too

many violent films with my dad?' he asked his little grey friend.

'Maybe!' cried Silvio. 'Possibly?' he said, more quietly. 'I don't know. Am I?'

Aubrey laughed. 'They're not for silverfish, are they? They're for adults.'

'Like no kid ever watched a film with someone bashing someone in it,' Silvio scoffed. 'Why are we picking on silverfish here?'

'Excuse me,' Villi said, in her low whirring voice. 'I hate to interrupt, but who are you guys? Some sort of film club? Or are you mugging me?'

FOOTNOTE: Villi did this by contracting her abdomen – like you tensing your tummy muscles – which drew her breath into her through holes in it, called spiracles. Spiracles miracles! That's like you breathing through your armpits.

'No! No!' Aubrey cried, embarrassed.

'We're so sorry!' Silvio said. 'Not at all!"

'So who are you?'

Aubrey hesitated. 'We're trying to stop something bad,' he said.

'We're Warriors for Peace!' Silvio cried.

'We've heard Big B is going to do something terrible and we're trying to stop him,' Aubrey said. 'And you know who he is.'

The hornet slowly shook her magnificent little head.

'Warriors for Peace,' she said slowly. 'Some- one has been winding you up. I've never heard of Big B. And I've never eaten a silverfish. Yet.' She studied the two friends. 'Peace Warriors?' she said again. 'Wouldn't the world be a safer place if you stayed at home playing on your phones?'

And with that she flew off, buzzing away in a dignified straight line.

Aubrey and Silvio's eyes met.

'That was a bit waspish,' Aubrey said.

'That stung!'

'Waspish!' Silvio screamed, and they both got terrible giggles.

'There's no way you're having a phone,' Aubrey said to the silverfish. 'Don't even think about it.'

CHAPTER 8
Terrible Spiders

On Saturday morning Mr Greenwood was in his barn with a pitchfork. He was determined to make money today – with any luck, a lot of money. If that meant pricking some of his cows in the bum with the sharp points of his pitchfork then, Mr Greenwood felt, that was just tough luck on those cows.

Since the Great Animal Rebellion began the price of meat had more than doubled and doubled again. Instead of paying six pounds for a steak, some people were now prepared to pay over twenty-five. Restaurants were charging over fifty. This meant that if Mr Greenwood could get a few of his cows into the back of his lorry and off to market he could very quickly make more money in one trip than he had ever made before.

Farming is not a get-rich-quick kind of profession normally, and the thought of the thousands of pounds he could earn had Mr Greenwood leaping out of bed this fine morning. He was prepared to stick his pitchfork into some cow rumps pretty hard if that is what he had to do. The pitchfork made him feel big and powerful. Suddenly he was not just a farmer any more. He was a dangerous warrior with a weapon.

'Right,' Mr Greenwood said to the cows (he had tricked them into the shed with some tasty fodder and feed nuts, even though it was high summer and there was plenty of grass in the meadows). 'Get up that ramp and into that truck. You're going to market. Fly! Get them going!'

Fly, his sheepdog, immediately sat down.

'Fly!' he shouted. 'Get out by!'

Fly put her head on one side, licked her lips and thumped her tail on the ground.

'Move, you useless dog!' Mr Greenwood roared.

Fly lay down and wagged her tail. The dog was a committed member of the Great Animal Rebellion. She was not planning to chase any cows.

'Argh!' screamed Mr Greenwood. He aimed a kick at her. She dodged him easily and sat down again.

The cows lowed in mild alarm. It distressed them to see their farmer losing his temper.

'Shoo, cows!' Mr Greenwood shouted. His face was very red.

The cows fled from him, mooing loudly.

'Get in that lorry!'

'Moo! Moo!'

'Move you stupid animals! Up that ramp or I'll spike you!'

Cows and man ran helter-skelter round the

inside of the barn. Fly joined in. She barked at Mr Greenwood. Mr Greenwood began to lash out with his pitchfork.

A pitchfork is a tool with a long wooden handle like a broom – but instead of a brush, a pitchfork ends in two sharp metal points. It is a fearsome instrument made for picking up bundles of hay. In medieval times people who felt they needed a weapon, but could not afford to buy swords or maces, often used pitchforks. It is like the polar bear and rifle situation: if you haven't got one and the other guy has, you are in trouble. (Polar bears with rifles do not bear thinking about.)

There was nothing the cows could do except moo and run and try to stay out of Mr Greenwood's way. Mr Greenwood succeeded in jabbing two cows with his pitchfork, on their rumps, which are the fatty bit of a cow's backside. The animals cried out but still they did not run up the ramp into the lorry.

The farm jackdaws, who passed on every bit of news about the rebellion to all the animals they knew, had explained to the cows that entering the lorry would mean being turned into steaks and burgers. The cows were determined to avoid this.

Beyond anger, a state in which people make mistakes, lies fury. Beyond fury lies rage, a state in which people make very serious mistakes. Raging Mr Greenwood was beginning to think he should throw his pitchfork at one of the cows, as if he were an expert hunter of the Kalahari, rather than an out-of-control farmer with a red face.

Suddenly he knew he was being watched. He looked up, panting harshly. In the doorway he could see a small figure. The sun was shining into the barn; the glare made it hard to see clearly but there was definitely a figure there.

Mr Greenwood stopped.

The cows stopped.

Fly had already stopped.

'Who's there?' Mr Greenwood shouted.

There was a sudden silence. The panting of cows could be heard, along with the panting of Mr Greenwood.

'What do you want?'

The small figure said nothing. It appeared to be manipulating something in its hands, something like an X-Box controller – or was it a phone?

Mr Greenwood saw something falling to his right, and something else to his left, and whatever they were they hit the barn floor with two soft thumps. Mr Greenwood jumped back. Now it was his turn to shout in fear.

Two enormous spiders, bigger than

anything he had even seen on television, were rushing at him.

The spiders were the size of a large child's shoes.

The spiders were black and red, with markings on them like small golden lights which seemed to flash.

Mr Greenwood stabbed downwards with his pitchfork, but the terrible spiders were too close to him and he missed. They sprang from about a foot away and landed on his legs. The jaws of one sunk into his right Wellington boot. The rubber protected him as he yelled and tried to slap the other off, but with horrible speed it climbed his left leg and bit him on the thigh. Mr Greenwood howled, and not from pain; the spider's jaws were so sharp he barely felt more than a scratch. He howled in horror.

The next second the spiders had dropped off him and scuttled away. They dashed across the barn, ignoring the cows, heading for the little figure standing in the glaring sunlight.

Mr Greenwood felt extremely peculiar. He felt bizarre and odd. It seemed to him that the small figure picked up the two spiders. Now the figure vanished. Mr Greenwood was alone in the barn with the cows, who were watching him curiously, and Fly, who was studying him with her head on one side.

He dropped his pitchfork.

By themselves, it seemed, Mr Greenwood's arms raised themselves above his head like a ballet dancer's. He stamped on the floor, first with his left foot, then with his right. His hips did a groovy circle. His shoulder rocked and jiggled. His knees bent and began to pump.

'Acha-acha-acah—oohh, baby!' Mr Greenwood uttered. 'Yeaah! Oooh-wee! OOOOooh HUP! Hup-HUP! Ooooh yeah, ah-ha! I wanna dance!'

Mr Greenwood's feet began to switch back and forth in time. He grooved across the barn, his hands making wild but matching moves in the air around him. It was as though he was listening to loud dance music that none of the cows could hear. It was as though he was in the middle of a disco and Whitney Houston was singing 'I Wanna Dance With Somebody' just for him.

Now, the extraordinary happened. If you had been watching, you would have thought that Mr Greenwood had spent his whole life touring night clubs and dances, learning the best moves from all over the world and perfecting them. He may not have been the best farmer on earth but suddenly Mr Greenwood had become, in his own mind at least, one of the world's slickest dancers. He found he was doing the Twist.

'Come On Everybody!' he shouted to the amazed cows. 'Let's Twist Again!'

Round and round and up and down, Mr Greenwood did the twist. Now he did the Swim. Now he did the Bird. Next he was shouting at Fly, who was hardly able to breathe for surprise.

'Hammer Time! Come on, Fly!'

Mr Greenwood's legs were doing amazing floppy sorts of splits.

Fly barked encouragement. The cows mooed with glee at seeing someone they had thought a rather horrid, bad-tempered bully transformed into a man who was dancing for sheer delight.

Mr Greenwood seemed to have found his purpose in life. He did the Mashed Potato. He did the Swing and he did the Bogle. He Pushed the Button and Slip-slided. He performed the Charleston, the Tango, the Tip-toe, the Rhumba and the Jump Around. When Mrs Greenwood came to look for him she gazed in amazement. Her husband was breaking it down with a series of flic-flacs, hip-hops, body-pops and back-beats.

'Dudley! What are you doing?' she yelled. (Mrs Greenwood liked yelling.)

'Get down, baby! Get on the floor!' Mr Greenwood retorted.

'Stop! Stop now!'

'Freak out, baby!' Mr Greenwood cried. He was holding his right foot in his right hand

and cupping the back of his neck with his left while making kick-jumping moves.

'Jive, baby!'

'What's got into you?'

'I'm Rhumba! I'm Tango! I'm the Spirit of Mambo!'

'I'm calling the police,' Mrs Greenwood replied.

'Groove is in the heart!' Mr Greenwood yipped in a peculiar high voice.

'Police, please,' Mrs Greenwood said into her mobile.

'Police emergency,' said the phone. 'How can I help you?'

'My husband has gone insane,' Mrs Greenwood said.

'What is the problem, exactly?'

'The problem exactly is he's as mad as an earwig. He won't stop dancing.'

'Are you in any danger?'

'I'm in danger of slapping him!'

'Can you describe what he's doing?'

'I doubt it. What are you doing, Dudley?'

'Walk like an Egyptian!' gasped Mr Greenwood.

All this dancing was tiring. He was presently slow-walking, bent-kneed, with one hand flat in front of him making pecking movements while the other did the same behind him and his head rocked back and forth like a crazy duck.

'He's in the barn with the cows and he's doing dances – dances he doesn't even know! He's never danced – he could have a heart attack!'

'Is he dancing with anyone?'

'It's the Bangles, baby!' Mr Greenwood called. 'They're right here with me.'

'Just the cows. He's calling them the Bangles. And the dog.'

The emergency police operator sounded surprised and slightly amused. 'So – we've got a farmer dancing with the Bangles, which are actually cows, and a dog? And he's been doing it all morning in his barn and you're worried he might be a danger to himself?'

'He needs help,' said Mrs Greenwood.

'I think our officers might like to take a look at this,' said the operator, who might have been trying not to laugh. 'There's a car on the way. Try to get him to drink some water and sit down.'

By the time the police arrived, Mr Greenwood was all danced out. He sat down quietly, panting. Mrs Greenwood made the two police officers cups of tea. Mr Greenwood fell asleep before he had taken a sip of his. The police said they thought he would be alright now, and they drove away. Mrs Greenwood let the cows go back to their field. She gave Fly her supper.

The jackdaws reported the news that two strange spiders had cured Mr Greenwood of his pitchfork rage.

'Farmer dances for peace!' they told the world. And indeed, when Mr Greenwood woke up, he seemed like a changed man.

'I don't want to mistreat animals ever again,' he told Mrs Greenwood. 'I am going to stop using pesticides and herbicides. I am going to lead a Green Life.'

Somewhere not far away the small figure known to the animals as Big B heard the news and smiled.

'The test has worked,' the small figure told the crowd of Terrible Spiders gathered around them. 'We have the power. They will all dance, and the world will never be the same again. When the wasps have done their job, we will be ready to strike. Tonight you will move to your attack positions. Prepare to save the world!'

Below the small figure, the Terrible Spiders clicked their jaws and tapped their feet in excitement. The noise of so many of them clicking and tapping together was like an enormous rattling storm of hail. Their eyes glowed green. The yellow markings on their thoraxes shone. They looked like a sea of tiny lights.

Now the small figure turned to a wasp which had landed nearby.

'You know what to do,' the small figure said. 'Tomorrow is the Day of the Wasps. Pass the message. Begin your work at first light.'

The wasp bobbed its head obediently and flew off.

All was peaceful on Woodside Terrace. Aubrey, Silvio and Ariadne were planning in the attic.

'Lucky you didn't kill that hornet,' Silvio said. 'She'd never heard of Big B.'

'Lucky I didn't listen to you!' said Aubrey.

'If we're going back to the wasps' nest

we'll need to be in position before they get up,' Ariadne said.

'Too right we're going back,' said Aubrey. 'I have been chased by wasps twice, stung by wasps three times, and tricked by a wasp I thought respected me into fighting a hornet I actually liked, in the end.'

Later on, Aubrey surprised Suzanne and Jim by going to bed soon after supper. Ariadne went hunting around the dark corners of the house and slept in her web in the corner of the skylight. Silvio finished off a biscuit crumb he had been saving and curled up to sleep.

CHAPTER 9
The Eve of Battle

Every day begins at midnight when most of the world we know is fast asleep.

Now, while we dream deep in our soft beds, another world, the world of the night, takes over. Great ships unload their cargoes in ports we never see. In the ports, lines of trains and trucks collect all the goods our daily lives require, from sofas to tomatoes, umbrellas to computers, pencils to peaches and bananas to bedspreads.

Great tides of food and wares are hauled inland by lorries and taken to warehouses, those huge sheds with no names on them that you sometimes see near motorways. Here everything is counted and sorted and reloaded onto more trucks and tankers.

Now the motorways thrum with the slow

lines of heavy lorries, carrying everything
to the shops.

This system is called the supply chain and
every night it prepares the sleeping world
for the day to come.

Nocturnal animals know all about this
other world, and the small, determined
figure of Big B knew all about it too. While

the valley slept, the Terrible Spiders made for their attack positions.

Big B had identified a weak point in the supply chain: a warehouse. Like a scuttling tide, the Terrible Spiders dashed through the night, heading for this huge shed on the edge of the motorway. In through the air ducts and drains they went, across the ceilings, through the entrances and exits, making for the crates of foods and goods which were due to be delivered throughout Aubrey's valley. Into the crates and the containers they crept and burrowed, hiding themselves among the world's wares.

Now the trucks and the trailers and the lorries came and lifted and loaded and carried and drove them. Now the unloaders worked for them, wheeling out the crates, unpacking the containers, carrying the hidden spiders into all the shops and supermarkets of the valley. Big B had chosen carefully: by the time the dawn came most of the shops in the valley had received deliveries containing something the size of a large child's shoe, something black, red, yellow and hairy.

If you had been awake that early summer morning and sitting very still at the end of the Ferrabys' garden, you might have seen three wasps perching on a bramble briar not far from their nest. The Guard Captain was briefing her two troops.

'Big day today,' she said. 'The biggest ever. Are your stings sharp? Are you ready for more action than you have ever seen or heard about?'

'Sure we are!' replied the first wasp, whose friends called him Vizzy. 'What do we have to do again?'

'Don't you listen to anything?' buzzed the other, whose friends knew him as Zivvy. 'Do you really pay no attention at all?'

'You know I don't,' Vizzy replied. 'I've got you to do that for me.'

'I thought I had you!' Zivvy exclaimed. 'I wasn't listening. It was your turn to do that. I was thinking about something else. I was thinking about jam.'

'You're always thinking about jam! You're a disgrace. You don't deserve to be a Guard.'

'Well if I don't you definitely don't. I should sting you.'

'Sting me! I'll sting you, you part-time shambles of an insect.'

'Oh, go on then! Go on! See what happens! I'll sting...'

'Right!' yelled the Guard Captain. 'Here are your orders, straight from Big B at Hollins Hall. Today is the Day of the Wasp. We are going on the offensive. In the past we have only stung people if they hit us, scared us or came too near our nests. But not today. Today we are going out to sting.

Everyone aged eighteen or below is going to get stung. It's going to be hard and dangerous, but we're wasps. We're not scared of anything. Today is going to be a great day in history, and we're going to be right in the middle of it.'

Vizzy and Zivvy looked at each other, then they both stared at the Guard Captain.

'We've never done this before? Wasps have never done this before?' Zivvy asked.

'And now we're suddenly going to start stinging people who haven't done anything to us? Children?' said Vizzy, doubtfully.

'That's right,' said the Guard Captain, uncomfortably. She drew herself up to her full tiny height. 'I repeat,' she said, 'those are our orders from Hollins Hall. An army can't survive if we don't obey our orders.'

Zivvy and Vizzy looked as unimpressed as wasps can look. They showed no sign of even having heard the Guard Captain. They stared at her.

'What's the problem?' she demanded.

'Those are the worst orders I can imagine,' said Zivvy.

'They suck,' Vizzy agreed. 'I mean, I like stinging, of course I do. It's my job. But I sting for a reason.'

'Me too!' Zivvy cried.

'I sting for the common good. I sting so that the whole nest can live safe and busy lives. But just going out and stinging a load of kids – that's wrong. The humans will hate us.'

'That's what I think,' Zivvy added, eagerly.

'They'll come to get us!' Vizzy exclaimed. 'They'll burn us out. They'll spray us. It will be the end of us.'

'I agree,' Zivvy said. 'These orders are nuts.'

'Do you two love humans or what?' the Guard Captain demanded.

'They're alright,' said Vizzy.

'They're just humans,' Zivvy said.

Now it was the Guard Captain's turn to look amazed. She buzzed ferociously.

'These are the same humans who have poisoned the air, polluted the oceans, melted the ice caps, killed the birds, wiped out the insects, hunted the animals, filled the earth with rubbish and the seas with plastic. Those humans? We are talking about the same humans?'

The other two looked thoughtful. Zivvy looked at the bramble bush. Vizzy studied the sky. The Guard Captain continued.

'I just want to be sure you don't mean a whole different set of humans I've never heard of. I mean, if you two know a race of humans who treasure the planet, who protect insects and animals and birds, who love the seas and the air and the forests and the jungles – if that's who you mean, could you show me where they live? Because I definitely wouldn't want to sting any of them.'

Zivvy looked at Vizzy. 'She's got me there,' he said.

'I accept that humans aren't that great,' Vizzy said. 'When you put it like that. But they do basically leave us alone. How is stinging their kids going to help? Aren't the kids the ones we should be making friends with? And it's not the kids who start the damage, is it? They probably don't want to kill the earth any more than we do. Surely it's not them we should be stinging, but their parents? If you gave me two humans, one a young one, the other an old one, and said, sting the one that's done the most damage, I definitely wouldn't sting the kid!'

Zivvy looked at Vizzy with great admiration.

'He's got you there,' he said to the Guard Captain.

The Guard Captain flexed her wings and pushed out her sting a little, like someone warming up for some action.

'We're not stinging them because we want to fight them,' she said. 'We're stinging them to help them.'

'Help them! How?' cried Vizzy.

'That's what I was going to ask,' Zivvy said.

'The Terrible Spiders are in their attack positions. When Big B gives the signal they are going to strike. They're going to bite everyone and everyone they bite is going to dance until they can't dance anymore. The whole human world will stop. They won't be able to drive their polluting cars. They won't be able to fly their polluting planes. Their factories and power stations will stop working. And when they've finished dancing, they are just going to want to go home, see their friends and families, and do good simple things like cooking and gardening and home improvements. Just like us – they'll do all the little jobs they've been putting off. They will visit their grandparents and have the neighbours round when they can. For some reason we don't understand, dancing makes humans better people. We know this because that farmer, Greenwood, has changed his life. He is looking after the soil, and he's not using pesticides. He's much nicer to his animals. He never uses a pitchfork on the cows anymore. He is still farming but he is farming with care.'

'So why are we stinging the children?' Vizzy asked.

'Great question!' Zivvy cried. 'Why?'

'Because if they have been stung by a wasp, the Terrible Spiders' bites will have no effect on them. They will hardly feel it. They will be immune. They won't dance. They will be themselves. And then it will be up to them how they live; they will be the second chance for the whole world and for all humans. Big B says it will be a new world for all of us, or at least the chance of one.'

'Well,' said Zivvy. 'I don't know what to think of that.'

'I'm just not sure about stinging kids,' Vizzy said.

'We could just sting them and see?' Zivvy said, slyly. 'It is what we're good at, isn't it? Imagine it – WASPS SAVE THE WORLD! That's the kind of news anyone would enjoy, isn't it? I'm IN!'

'But they're going to fight back, aren't they?' Vizzy objected. 'When a wasp stings a human, that wasp often gets squished. I don't mind fighting to protect our nest, but I don't want to die today. I like life!'

Sitting very still by the woodpile at the top of the Ferrabys' garden and listening to the wasps were three shapes you would have recognised. There was Aubrey, as still as a stone. There was a large spider next to him: Ariadne. And sitting on his shoulder waving his antennae in the air was a small bright silverfish: Silvio.

They sat very still, eavesdropping, and heard every word.

'How can we tell who to sting?' Vizzy asked. 'Do we sting babies? How will we know how old the children are – do we ask them? That's not going to work.'

'No babies,' said the Guard Captain. 'If they're not old enough to squish an insect, we leave them alone.'

'But the others all look the same to me,' Zivvy objected.

'School. If they're old enough to be in school, we sting them. If they're in school uniform, we sting them. If they ought to be in school but they're not – we sting them. It's easy,' said the Guard Captain. 'We sting them on the way to school, we sting them at break time and at home time.

That's three chances at every child, and we only have to get them once.'

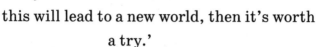

'Well, if you say so,' said Vizzy. 'If there is a chance this will lead to a new world, then it's worth a try.'

'It's going to be a lot of fun, in a way!' Zivvy exclaimed. 'Some of those children can be pretty horrible to insects. There are one or two I am going to enjoy stinging. And the rest – well, a sting doesn't hurt for very long. In the old days every child got stung; it was part of growing up. They'll get over it.'

'Well,' marvelled the Guard Captain. 'That's the longest speech I've ever heard from you. This is a remarkable day already. Are you ready?

Shall we get on with it? Shall we be the ones who start the Day of the Wasp?'

'Who's first?' asked Vizzy. 'Not Aubrey again?'

'No, he's been stung,' the Guard Captain said. 'Big B wanted to make sure. We can miss him out. There are other children on Woodside Terrace. Let's get into position on the gutters, so we can get them when they come out for school.'

With that, the three wasps took to the air.

CHAPTER 10
Big B

Ariadne was the first to speak.
'Wow! Wasp Apocalypse! That will teach people to splat all their house spiders... Actually, it probably won't.'

'Stung on Big B's orders from Hollins Hall,' Aubrey said. 'Why me?'

'They're going to war!' Silvio cried. 'Madness! The humans will go berserk. It's not just the wasps they'll come for! No insect will be safe. We've got to stop them.'

'How can we stop them?' Aubrey muttered. His head was spinning with what he had just heard.

'Do we even want to stop them?' Ariadne asked. 'Speaking as a spider – well, a lot of what Big B is doing is right. Imagine if it works. A world in which the humans stop destroying and start helping – it would be … it would be – wonderful!'

'I don't want Mum and Dad to get bitten by weird spiders and dance until they fall down!' Aubrey cried. 'They spend their lives looking after me, and you, actually, even though they're scared of spiders – and they don't mind silverfish in the kitchen. And the Ferrabys never did anything about this wasps' nest; they don't deserve this. Big B has gone too far. Children will be terrified. Everyone will be terrified. Everything could just fall apart.'

'Everything is falling apart,' Ariadne said, gently. 'Everyone knows it. What that wasp said about the oceans and the forests and the air and the soil and the animals is true. Humans know it better than anyone, and yet they just carry on.'

'Good humans are trying to help. Millions of people care about the planet,' Aubrey objected. 'This is a terrible way to treat them.'

'But there aren't enough of them, or they haven't got enough power,' Ariadne replied, tapping her eight feet impatiently. 'It's as though they are waiting for a miracle, waiting for someone to come along and change everything. Now someone has come along.'

'It's wrong,' Aubrey said. 'People are going to get hurt. And how do we know where it will stop? Suppose Big B is a lunatic who wants to take over the world?'

'That often happens in films,' Silvio put in. 'It's normally a madman who wants to do something massive and terrible and you have to stop them. That's kind of what I have been training for – me and Jim. The heroes have to stop big baddy.'

'But maybe Big B is the real hero!' Ariadne exclaimed. 'Have you thought of that?'

'We're the heroes,' Silvio said. 'I just know we are.'

'If we manage to stop a lot of people getting stung by wasps, bitten by oddball spiders, going mad and dancing until they fall down, we still might not be the heroes?' Aubrey asked Ariadne.

'What's more important, the world, planet Earth, or a bit of stinging and dancing?' Ariadne returned. 'A lot of animals and children would say the world.'

Aubrey looked thoughtful. 'What would the children want us do to? That's a good question. It is going to be their world. Big B is right about that. So – what would they want?'

'They'd want some action!' Silvio cried. 'I know they would!'

'There's going to be action whatever happens,' Aubrey told him. 'But they wouldn't want to get stung, that's for sure.'

'They might! If you said, "Would you get stung by a wasp to save the world?" a lot of kids would say, "OK!"' said Ariadne.

'They'd want to meet Big B,' said Silvio, with certainty. 'That's what we have to do.'

'Agree,' Ariadne said. 'I'm not sure if I want to stop Big B or join up but I definitely want to meet him, or her. Or them.'

Aubrey said, 'We've got about an hour before mum and dad get up and start looking for me. Time to get to Hollins Hall if we're quick.'

'Go!' cried Ariadne and scampered up his arm to his shoulder. 'Hit it!' shouted Silvio, and leapt onto Aubrey's hand, dropping from there into his pocket. 'Let's do this – whatever it is!'

The little boy scrambled over the fence at the top of the Ferrabys' garden and plunged into Rushing Wood. There was a beautiful cool feeling of shade. He smelled the sweet scent of a summer morning, the earth rich with promise and the trees bright in their leaves.

The path to Hollins Hall was a good one, running across a field everyone called Frieda's Field (it was particularly beloved of a black Labrador named Frieda, who could often be found rolling in mud and cow dung there) down a steep bank, across a fallen tree which bridged the stream and up the other side.

It was on the fallen tree, halfway across, as he trod as carefully as a tightrope walker with the torrent of the beck below him, that Aubrey met the Terrible Spider.

The thing came out of the undergrowth on the opposite bank and advanced towards him along the fallen tree. He stopped dead. The spider was as big as a small plate, black and bristly, with bright yellow markings which seemed to shine like lights.

A sound of fear and disgust came out of
Aubrey, something like, 'Uurk!'

The spider kept coming.

'What do you want?' Aubrey shouted at it.

No reply. The spider slowed but still
came on, at a stealthy pace now. There was
something horribly sinister about the way it
moved, Aubrey felt, like a robot.

'Fight it!' squeaked
Silvio.

'Run! Go back!'
cried Ariadne. 'It's
not natural, there's
something wrong
with it.'

'No! We said we were going to Hollins
Hall.'

Aubrey's heart was pounding now but he
was determined. He could not turn and run,
not with children about to be stung and
adults about to be bitten. He wrenched at a
slender branch and snapped it off: the stick

was as long as a cricket bat but thinner and whippier. 'Get out of the way, spider, you won't stop me!' he shouted.

His voice had no effect. The spider was only a metre away, tensing its legs.

'Come on then!' Aubrey roared, partly to give himself courage. 'Come and fight!'

The spider sprang at him. It jumped forward and high, as high as Aubrey's chest.

'SAH!' Aubrey yelled and swung his stick like a tennis racket. He struck the spider in mid-air – WHACK!

It was a perfect hit, catching the spider in full flight and sending it spinning sideways, cartwheeling through the air and down with a splash into the beck.

'YAH!' Aubrey shouted, with a surge of victory and relief, but then Ariadne was yelling, 'Look out! Behind you!' and Silvio was squealing in alarm and even as the boy turned another spider was rushing at him along the fallen tree. It was too close and too fast, Aubrey thought desperately, even as he swung the stick again. But he was off balance. He missed. The spider leaped, low and cleverly, landing on his left leg.

'YEEK!' Aubrey screamed, whacking at his attacker with the stick. The spider nipped him, biting right through his trousers. Its jaws were so sharp the boy felt more shock and disgust than pain. He struck the horrid thing, knocking it onto its back on the tree trunk. Without thinking he stamped on it, hard.

There was a splatty crack as the spider burst open, but instead of a splurge of goo and gunk, which you would expect inside an insect that size, there was an odd poppy crackling.

'Wires!' Aubrey cried. 'It's a robot.'

'Did it bite you?' Ariadne asked.

'Definitely,' Aubrey said, grimly. He crossed the tree to the other side and sat down on the grassy bank. He rolled up his trouser leg. There were the bite marks, two small red spots close together.

'Do you feel like dancing?' Silvio asked.

'No.'

'Sure?' Ariadne put in. 'You don't feel like doing the Floss?'

'No.'

'Do you fancy a quick Dab? A Twist? A waltz?'

'I really don't.'

'You're sure you don't want a spot of the tango?' Ariadne enquired.

'NO! I don't want to dance. I want to meet Big B.'

'Well good morning!' came a shout from the top of the bank. Aubrey turned and there was his father, Jim, looking foolish in running gear (he had just taken up running), sweating and grinning.

'You're up early! Time for breakfast, come on!'

'But, Dad...'

'Pancakes!' called Jim. 'Best thing about running is big breakfasts, and it's time to get ready for school.'

'But, Dad!'

'No buts! Get your little butt up here; I'll race you back to the house.'

'But I have to...'

'Save the world again? Sure, sure, so do we all. But we'll do it better with breakfast inside us, after we've been to school. Let's go! Up and at 'em!'

With a sigh, Aubrey did as he was told.

There was nothing to stop the Day of the Wasp now, he thought, but then a loud squawking came from the trees above him.

'Good work!' croaked a harsh, cawing voice. 'After a fight like that you deserve breakfast! Take it easy and put your feet up!'

It was Corone, the carrion crow, and he was looking down at Aubrey with great mischief. Aubrey suddenly felt a surge of determination. Corone was right – he had had a dramatic morning already, and he had survived it, and there was more to do. This was no time to be going for breakfast.

'I'll go back through the wood, Dad,' he called up the slope. 'See you in a bit.'

'OK!' Jim called back. 'I need to do my five kilometres. Don't be late back. You need to eat something before school!'

He set off one way and Aubrey set off the other, battling uphill towards Hollins Hall, through bushes and undergrowth, panting and climbing. It was not far to the hall if you went in a straight line but when he emerged in the yard of the big house he was covered in burrs, leaves and twigs, like a small version of the Green Man*.

The farm and its outbuildings looked deserted but for one horse, a beautiful black mare, which gazed at them over her stable door. Aubrey knew some of the children from school lived up here, in the cottages behind the farm, but none of them were about this early in the morning.

FOOTNOTE: The Green Man is a wonderful figure from European myth. He is the spirit of the woods and the wild, a great big sort of God fellow with wild hair and a tangled beard who represents rebirth, the coming of spring, and everything strange and beautiful and unknowable about nature, the forests and the hills.

'It's very quiet,' he said. 'Where would you be if you were Big B?'

'A secret bunker under the house?' Silvio suggested.

'A lair in a cave?' said Ariadne

'If B is a child like me then I doubt it will be lairs or bunkers,' Aubrey said. 'Where would you make Terrible Spiders?'

'I'd make them in there,' said Ariadne, nodding towards the barn. 'Spiders love barns.'

The old barn was surrounded by nettles. Its roof was corrugated iron, rusted red in patches. The doors were wooden, peeling with flaked paint. They were padlocked shut.

'No one has been in there for ages,' Silvio observed. 'Look at the nettles. It's abandoned.'

'It's the right size, though,' Aubrey said.

'It's huge. It's the perfect place. Let's check it.'

'I can get in easily,' Ariadne said. 'Put me down.'

She scuttled in between the nettles and vanished under the door.

'Let's try the back,' Silvio suggested. Aubrey nodded and circled around to the end of the building. It was like a huge stone ship, riding high above the summer valley. The sun was coming up and in the woods below all the birds were singing.

'It's beautiful,' he said. 'Mum loves running up here.'

At the end of the barn he climbed an old gate.

'Windows,' said Silvio, 'but too narrow for a human.'

They kept going and came to the back of the barn.

'There!'

A faint path, narrow and only just visible,

led through the nettles to a small door. It was ajar, but just a crack, not wide enough for an adult but Aubrey thought he might squeeze through. He did. At first he could see very little, but as his eyes adjusted he could make out huge stack of old hay bales, running from one side of the barn to the other.

'Nothing?' Silvio whispered.

'I'm not sure,' Aubrey whispered back. 'Someone's been coming and going – look.'

There was a faint path in the dust on the floor. Aubrey followed it. The path led to a point in the pile of hay bales. There was the softest tap on Aubrey's head as Ariadne let herself down from a beam.

'It gives me the creeps,' she whispered, and dived into his pocket.

'Something's here,' he whispered.

'Spooky!' Silvio hissed. 'Weird vibes!'

'I feel it too. Let's just try...'

Aubrey pushed at a gap between two of the

hay bales. His hand plunged straight into nothingness. 'I think I can get through,' he said.

The hay was old and musty. Aubrey covered his mouth with his sleeve; he knew old hay could be dangerous – its dust can inflame your lungs. He bent his head down to shield his face and pushed forward. There was a way through, dark and dusty, with bales pushing in on him from both sides and above, but he was in a tunnel of some kind. Although he was scared he took a firm grip on his stick and kept going.

Now the tunnel narrowed, forcing Aubrey to bend right down, and then with a stumble he was out. He stood up, light from the slit windows making the great space of the barn visible, and he took in the extraordinary sight before him.

On one side of the barn was a long workbench, on which three computers were linked together, their screens divided into dozens and dozens of little squares, all showing different pictures. The rest of the barn was filled with ranks of stacked hay bales, like rows of seats in an amphitheatre.

The bales were covered with Terrible Spiders. There must have been hundreds of them, lined up like toys in a huge warehouse. None of the spiders reacted to him. They sat still. He felt hundreds of spider eyes looking at him. He saw hundreds of legs all bent, tensed as if ready to jump.

'Holy Peter!' Silvio whispered.

Very slowly and very carefully, Aubrey took a step backwards. He was too amazed to have much of a plan – back down the tunnel and away as fast as possible was all he could think. Just as he was about to turn and run there was a commotion in the hay behind him and a small figure pushed out of the tunnel. Dressed neatly in school uniform, glasses polished bright, and carefully brushing hay off her cardigan, the small figure said, 'Hey Aubrey! What do you think of my spiders?'

It was Edie Morris.

CHAPTER 11
Edie Morris

'Edie! What – why – how – wh...?'
But before he had come up with a question, Aubrey knew the answer.

'You're not ... you are?'

He did not need to complete that one either. There was no answer possible except the one standing in front of him.

'Big B?' he asked, finally.

'I didn't think Small Edie would be quite as impressive,' Edie said.

'It's a good name,' Aubrey admitted. 'You can understand animals too?'

'Yes. They've told me all about your adventures,' Edie said. 'You're a hero to them. And to me actually.'

'And you had me stung because I can talk to animals?'

'Yes, and because you're brave, and if there was one person who would understand I knew it would be you.'

She did not blush or seem in any way embarrassed. In fact, Edie seemed very relaxed and quite amused. She was a different person at home, Aubrey realised. Lots of children were, but then no other child, as far as he knew, felt at home in charge of several thousand Terrible Spiders, which were still watching them.

'Is it all true? About the dancing?'

'It works brilliantly,' Edie said. 'It's a bit dramatic at first but when people get used to it they will be fine. They dance a lot and then they rethink their priorities.'

'How did you do it?'

'I needed to adjust human hormones with something more maternal; it's not enough to care for your young – you need to see that caring for the planet and the creatures is also caring for your own children. In the end I used sheep hormones. Ewes are amazingly protective of their lambs. Did you know that? And lambs love to skip and dance. It took a lot of experiments, but I got it in the end.'

'And the spiders?'

'They're just robots. I used parts from cheap drones and algorithms I got off the internet. That was easy.'

'And the wasps?'

'They signed up straight away. Pretty well every insect I've talked to is with us.'

'With us?'

'Aren't you with me, Aubrey? It's for the world you want – a world with creatures in it. We can't survive if we lose the creatures. There's no choice really.'

Edie looked at him earnestly, her eyes studying him.

'If I could have thought of another way I would have done – but at least this way works. Everyone wants to save the world, everyone good does, anyway – so I just went ahead and did the best I could.'

Aubrey laughed in amazement. 'I was expecting some sort of supervillain!' he said. 'I was ready for a fight!'

'Funny how so many stories want that sort of ending, isn't it?' Edie remarked. 'And yet those stories don't seem to help us at all. Everyone lives happily ever after and everything carries on like before. But we're running out of time, aren't we? It's now or never, isn't it?'

'Is it?'

'Have you heard of anyone else with a better plan?'

'Um...'

'Have you heard of anyone else with any kind of plan at all?'

'OK, no I haven't, not really. But Edie, all the adults dancing? Some of them will have heart attacks, won't they? Won't things crash and break and fall apart?'

'I guess,' said Edie. 'But adults say you can't make an omelette without breaking eggs.' She blinked. 'I guess that's true, even if they're the eggs!'

'Wow! Edie!'

'Why not? Isn't that reality? Don't we have to do the right thing, even if it's hard and not perfect? I mean – don't we, Aubrey? I love my parents and I like lots of adults, I just think they've had their chance and they're obviously not doing anything. So today we sting the kids – that gives them immunity. Tonight the spiders bite everyone – they're very simple robots – and by the end of tomorrow everyone will have danced, and they'll have a sleep, and the day after tomorrow, a better world! Around here, anyway. I'm only testing it on this valley at first. If it works, I'll put the instructions on the internet, send out more spiders and let other kids take over. Hey, have you had breakfast? Come and have something with my mum and dad. We can call yours and tell them you came by. Dad will drop you at your house after. Come on! Are you with me?'

Aubrey hesitated. Edie had given her ideas a lot of thought. He needed to think now, before he gave his answer. Food would be a good first step to the right answer, he knew.

'I'm with you on breakfast,' he said.

Edie led the way out of the barn. As they crossed the yard she swerved towards the stable where the black mare was looking out over her stable door. The horse whinnied in delight at the sight of Edie.

'This is Thunder,' she told Aubrey. 'Isn't she beautiful?'

'She is,' Aubrey answered. The mare dropped her nose for him, and he stroked it. The horse was enormous. Edie looked tiny beside her.

'She's the most wonderful thing in the world,' Edie breathed. 'And I'm her best friend.'

At breakfast Aubrey began to understand why Edie was not bothered at the thought of her parents being bitten by her spiders. They were very busy and quite stern. There was no laughter during the meal. Mr Morris made boiled eggs and toast. Mrs Morris made sure the children ate it quickly, crusts and all. Mr Morris asked if Edie had done her homework. Mrs Morris said Aubrey should ask his parents next time, before turning up for breakfast.

'A phone call would have been good,' she said. 'I've spoken to your parents. We'll take you to school with Edie.'

Mr and Mrs Morris made themselves smart for work. By the time they were in Mrs Morris's car, Aubrey was beginning to think that a bit of dancing would be good for them. In his house there was sometimes shouting... 'Come ON, Aubrey!' his father would bellow. 'Get your shoes on! You're moving like a dozy snail!' ...But there was always noise and talking nonsense and making jokes and laughter.

'Your parents are strict,' he whispered to Edie, in the back. Mr and Mrs Morris were in the front with the radio news on loudly.

'I know. They think it's best for me,' Edie said. 'It's no use telling them to lighten up; I've tried.'

'So you're not worried about them getting bitten and dancing?'

'Honestly,' Edie said, and she looked properly mischievous now, 'I can't wait!'

'But I don't want it to happen to my parents! I love them as they are. I don't know what your spiders are going to do to them. I'm not even sure you do. And being bitten is horrible. I think you have to stop it, Edie. You can't know what will happen. Things could get really badly out of control.'

'You are experiencing Fear of the Unknown,' said Edie, solemnly. 'It's very common. But it's just a sting or a nip and a bit of dancing. Nothing to worry about.'

Aubrey was not reassured.

Mrs Morris paused outside his house. Jim and Suzanne ran out and passed Aubrey's book bag into the car.

'Naughty child!' Jim shouted, smiling. 'I knew you wouldn't come home for breakfast. Wild boy of the woods! Have a happy day!'

'Have fun, darling!' Suzanne called. 'See you later! Love you!'

'Love you, Mum. Love you, Dad!' Aubrey called back.

It was quiet in the car then. Mr Morris turned up the news slightly.

'...mechanical spiders. Several of these drone spiders, as they are being called, have been found in a warehouse near the M62. A warehouse manager has been taken to hospital. Police are warning the public to report any sightings of these spiders, and not to approach them. Chief Inspector Mark Dashwood spoke to us a few minutes ago. "We are not in a position to disclose who may have made these drone spiders but my officers are investigating as a matter of urgency. We will identify the person or persons behind these alarming machines, and I am confident we will be making arrests shortly. We urge anyone with any information about drone spiders to contact us immediately."'

Aubrey looked at Edie, his eyes wide.

Edie winked.

'Hospital though!' Aubrey hissed. 'That's not supposed to happen, is it?'

'They weren't supposed to do anything until tonight,' Edie said, very quietly. 'Must have been a mistake. Never mind. That's omelettes for you.'

'Edie! People are not omelettes!'

'What are you two muttering about?' Mrs Morris asked.

'Nothing!' they said together, at once.

'Here we are,' said Mr Morris, as they pulled up and stopped down the road from the school gates. 'Off you go. Work hard. Get top marks in everything, Edie.'

'OK, Dad.'

'See you later.'

'Bye, Mum.'

'Bye bye, Edie. Do your best.'

'It looks like there's a rumpus by the school gate,' Mr Morris said. 'Don't get involved children – be good.'

The Morrises pulled away in their large car, then, so they did not see what was really happening around the gate and in the playground.

It was pandemonium.

Children were yelling and shouting. Parents and teachers were striking out wildly. Some adults were running back to their cars with their children. Others were sprinting for the safety of school.

'Wasps! Wasps!' they screamed.

'Edie!' Aubrey shouted, as they battled their way through a horde of panicked parents, howling children and zooming wasps. 'This is a terrible plan and it's going terribly wrong.'

'It will all make sense,' Edie returned, calmly. 'Everyone will be just fine when it's over.'

'They're not fine now!'

The headmistress came running past them carrying a child who looked about nine, who had been stung on the arm. The child was crying and shouting wildly.

'See? That's just making a fuss,' Edie said. 'By lunchtime he will have forgotten all about it.'

'No, Edie! Maybe you're right: heroes living happily ever after and everything carrying on the same as it was before is probably rubbish. But you can't make people change by stinging them and biting them. If you're going to carry on with this...'

Edie's eyes flashed.

'I am,' she said. 'You bet I am.'

'Right – I am going stop you!'

'You can try,' Edie said. 'Go right ahead

and try. I'd like it. I'd love a battle! Who've you got on your team? I have hundreds of robot spiders and all the wasps.'

'I've got one house spider and one silverfish,' Aubrey admitted. Suddenly he was grinning.

Edie laughed.

'Brilliant!' she cried. She clapped her hands. 'This is going to be the best battle ever! Shake hands?'

Aubrey shook her hand.

'Edie,' he said, 'I hope your spiders are beaten to bits.'

'Aubrey,' said Edie, 'I hope my spiders and wasps put people right and give them a lot of stings and bites to help them remember their lesson.'

'Done,' said Aubrey.

'Done.'

He needed time, and he needed help. Coolly, calmly and without hesitating, Aubrey smashed the glass cover on a fire alarm box. Immediately the alarm began clanging wildly.

'Mistake!' he shouted. 'It's not a fire! I hit it!'

While the teachers agreed that going outside was a bad idea and gathered the children in the hall, Aubrey slipped away. He held a quick conference with Silvio and Ariadne in the boys' cloakroom.

'What are wasps scared of?'

'Fly swats,' said Silvio. 'And flame throwers. Everything's scared of flame throwers.'

'That's no good to us.'

'Insect spray,' said Ariadne, 'and hornets. Wasps are not scared of much but they fear and respect hornets like you wouldn't believe. They almost revere them. Just because a thing is bigger than you and more powerful than you seems no reason to fear or respect it, but try telling wasps that.'

'We know a hornet!' Aubrey said. 'She seemed – um – well – she seemed pretty cool once she realised we weren't trying to mug her. Can you pass on the word?'

'I'll tell the woodlice who live behind the kitchen to tell the blue tits to tell the jackdaws,' Silvio replied. 'What's the message?'

'Tell her I am very sorry about the station thing and can we please speak? I'll meet her by the window to the toilets as soon as she can get there. Tell her the insects are depending on her.'

'On my way,' said Silvio.

'Are the insects really depending on this, Aubrey?' Ariadne asked.

When a large house spider asks you a direct question it certainly makes you think.

Aubrey looked fondly at his friend.

'If the Day of the Wasp gets worse the humans will wipe out the wasps, and the hornets. If Edie carries on with her plan she will be in trouble. We need to do this for the insects, the spiders, and for Edie. And for all the people she's planning to have bitten.'

Ariadne studied him with all her eyes.

'You are right about the insects,' she said, at last. 'And the spiders. We need the humans on our side. I'm not sure about the robot spiders. I was quite looking forward to seeing the humans learning a lesson.

They've been treating creatures terribly for too long.'

'Will you help me, Ariadne?'

'Ye-es. I will help you with the wasps, anyway. What do you need?'

'We need to create so much chaos in the classroom today that the teachers don't realise I'm not there. Or we need to somehow shut the school.'

Ariadne's eyes gleamed.

'That will be my pleasure,' she said. 'We could have some fun! I've never shut down a school before.'

'We have to wait until the hornet gets here before anyone goes outside,' Aubrey said.

'No problem, as Silvio would say,' Ariadne replied.

Aubrey hoped she was right. He could see another problem. How do you even begin to ask for help from someone – or some hornet – you have fought with? Someone who tried to hurt you, whom you tried to hurt? He would never forget it, and he was sure the hornet would not, either. He imagined he was the hornet. Someone who has knocked you out now wants a truce – wants your help!

What would I do? Aubrey thought. Would I get a load of other hornets and sting him all over? Would I tell him to buzz off? He wanted to ask Ariadne, 'How do you end a fight and start a friendship?' but she had already gone off to cause chaos.

CHAPTER 12

Fantastic Chaos

Aubrey had known for a long time that Ariadne was a wise and popular spider with many friends in the vast animal kingdom. He had had no idea quite how far her influence reached, however, until he asked her to use it. Ariadne and her friends did not just disrupt his class. They turned the whole school into a riot.

Her first move was house spiders, huge ones, which emerged from their various hiding places all over the school and charged the teachers. Most teachers turned out to be scared of large charging spiders. They yelped, jumped out of the way, shrieked (Mr Matthews, the science teacher, was particularly scared of spiders) and leapt up on their desks. That took a lot of time out of the lessons.

Next came the magpies. Twenty-five magpies turned up and landed on the windowsills. They tapped hard and rapidly on the glass and gave their rattling call:

'Chak chak chak chak!' they shouted, 'Chak chak chak!'

You can imagine the effect that had on lessons. More chaos. Some of the children threw balls of paper and pens at the windows. The magpies loved that, and shouted and tapped, encouraging them. Children yelled with excitement, magpies cackled and the teachers, already rattled, thought it would be a good idea to get the children into the hall again, where they could keep an eye on them.

The children were wildly over-excited and not learning from their lessons anyway. They were, however, learning a great deal about the powers of the animal kingdom.

While all this was going on it was easy for Aubrey to slip away again.

Edie watched him go, her eyes glinting. The battle was on!

Aubrey met Villi by the open window in the

lavatories. Aubrey had to stand on the loo seat. This brought him face-to-face with the hornet.

A hornet up close is a wonderful sight, like the most impressive Halloween pumpkin ever carved. Villi's dark eyes covered half of her face. Massive mandibles, which are like jaws turned on their sides, opened down the middle of what would be her chin, revealing chomping great cutters. Antennae which can smell, touch, sense movement and listen poked out of the top of her head. She even had bright dots like eyes on her forehead. Before he could stop himself, Aubrey said, 'Woah! Are those – extra eyes?'

Villi's antennae twitched.

'Sorry, that was very rude. I meant to say, I am so sorry that–'

'They are ocelli,' Villi said. 'Light sensors. They mean I can fly in near-darkness and detect shapes and movement.'

'How cool is that!' exclaimed the boy.

'Yes. If someone is trying to hit me or kick me, even in the dark, I can see every move!'

'I'm really sorry. I thought you were going to sting me.'

'I know. I thought you were going to swat me.'

Aubrey nodded. 'I was really excited and nervous so when you came at me I just...'

'Yes,' Villi agreed. 'I thought, "Oh here we go again, another one!" and so I got ready to fight.'

Villi smiled – and if you can imagine doing that with mandible jaws which run sideways down the middle of your face, you can imagine what a smile it was.

'I understand you need my help,' she said, 'with this plan of Big B's, which seems an excellent plan to me.'

'Yes! No! I mean, Big B's plan is going to get all the wasps and hornets killed. The humans will never forgive an attack on their children.'

'Way I hear it,' Villi said, 'all the humans are going to be danced out.'

'Only the ones in this valley!' Aubrey cried. 'On the news tonight they will be announcing an extermination plan for wasps and hornets all over the country. It will be the end of you! The Night of the Spiders will be too late for you – for all of you.'

Villi snapped her mandibles together.

'Drat,' she said.

'Exactly!' Aubrey exclaimed. 'But how do we stop the wasps?'

The hornet vibrated her wings slightly with pleasure. There is nothing a hornet likes so much as being asked for a plan in the heat of battle.

'We need to tell all the wasps to stop stinging people, and we need to do it before break time. That's two hours. We'll tell every bird, insect and animal to pass it on. Leave it to me. But what about the robot spider things?'

'They're programmed to attack humans. Animals will be quite safe...' Aubrey said. 'Would the animals help the humans?'

Villi looked hard at him. She was only very small compared to Aubrey, but she had a very direct look. She said, slowly, 'Get the animals to help get rid of the robot spiders? The robot spiders that are supposed to help them?'

Then she laughed and said quickly, 'It's a thought! Talk it through later, get some more heads on it? As soon as you can get there?'

'Sure!' Aubrey said. He felt a huge excitement running through him. There is nothing better than actually doing things, he felt. Talking about things and thinking about things are all very well, but nothing but nothing beats doing them.

'Ariadne says she's going to shut the school down. How long will it take you to call off the wasps?'

'Half an hour,' said Villi. 'I'd like to see a spider shut a school, but I've got business. See you later. Fight well!'

With a steady buzz she was gone.

Aubrey went back to the hall. Now the children were being sent back to their classrooms, the magpies having flown away. Ariadne was waiting for him discretely, keeping very still in his pencil case.

'Ready?'

'Villi said half an hour! What are you going to do?'

'We're going to close this place. Watch.'

Edie was looking at Aubrey across the classroom, smiling a mischievous smile and shaking her head slightly, as if to say, 'You'll never get away with it!'

Aubrey gave her a big wink. Ariadne

signalled to a large spider up on the ceiling, who waved her legs at a sparrow on the windowsill. The sparrow flew off, cheeping loudly.

And now came the rats.

Rats ran along windowsills. Rats dashed suddenly along corridors. Rats appeared and disappeared in the lavatories, the cloak rooms, on the stairs and even in the cupboards.

The children were taken to the hall again. Teachers armed with cricket bats and hockey sticks guarded the doors. The headmistress called the council. The council called the pest control officer. The Environmental Health officer became involved. Soon the school secretary was sending text alerts to all the parents. With so many rats around the school had been declared a Health Hazard. The children would have to go home for the rest of the day while the buildings were made safe.

'Cheeky humans!' said a voice from near Aubrey's foot. A grey rat with very bright eyes was looking up at him. 'We don't carry a tenth of the diseases you guys do,' it said. 'Enjoy your day off!'

The rat blinked at him in a comical way and was gone, dashing between amazed children, dodging the PE teacher, side-stepping the maths teacher, winking at the deputy head and disappearing smoothly into the staff room, from where there came a series of roars, squeals and shouts.

'Rats,' Ariadne sighed, 'are just the coolest animals. If the humans are ever wiped out, they'll take over. They always have a plan.'

The children poured into the yard. No wasps attacked them. Three small black and yellow insects observed them from a twig overlooking the playground.

'I'm ready to go again,' said Vizzy. 'I got

twelve of them this morning and only got swatted once.'

'I'm shattered,' Zivvy replied. 'I got nineteen! I should get a medal. A woman hit me quite hard but I just bounced off and went in again.'

'See how they're being careful now! Looking around everywhere, jumping at flies. They won't forget the Day of the Wasp!' said the Guard Captain.

'Why did we stop?'

'Orders. The message said the Queen said the hornets said we had to stop, or we'd provoke the humans to terrible vengeance.'

'The hornets said that?' Zivvy asked. 'Really? The hornets themselves? I love hornets! They're so – big! And so – orange! Oh, I'd love to be a hornet.'

'Do you think we did enough for Big B?' Vizzy asked.

'The hornets say we're done stinging – it's

back to the usual rules. Only near the nest or if they start it.'

'It's going to be a long summer,' said Zivvy, happily. 'We'll get loads of stinging in. We must have stung half the children in the valley.'

'The only question is,' Vizzy replied, thoughtfully, 'what happens to the other half when the Night of the Spiders starts later? Are they all going to dance the tarantella?'

'What do the hornets say?'

'They don't know either.'

'The hornets don't know?' Zivvy looked shocked. 'I've never heard anything like it! Let's go home.'

Edie ran up to Aubrey in the playground. 'What have you done?' she cried. 'Don't you see what you've done?'

'Round one to you – the Morning of the

Wasp. Round two to me – the Afternoon of Not the Wasp,' Aubrey returned.

'But the spiders! If the children who haven't been stung get bitten, they'll dance the tarantella too.'

'So? It was your crazy idea: robot spiders!'

'They're not meant to bite children. The whole point was to give the children a chance to lead, to have their say – not to have them dancing! I don't even know what happens to a child who gets bitten. It might be too strong for them. It might hurt them, Aubrey!'

'Edie. You are the most incredible scientist. But this plan was too dangerous. Call off the spiders. Back to base. Change of plan. No biting, no dancing. You've shown what you can do! The animals will always listen to you. I am sure you will change the world, but – not today. Call them off.'

Edie's eyes were full of alarm.

'But Aubrey,' she said. 'I can't call them

off. They only have one programme. I have set them up to wait in hiding until it gets dark, then to come out and attack.'

'You have no control over them at all?' Aubrey whispered. He was suddenly terrified.

'I can control their positions. I can move them to different attack points, but I can't stop them attacking.'

The two children were walking around the playground. Now they paused under a tree. Aubrey thought desperately. What to do? If Edie couldn't call the spiders off then by tomorrow morning half the valley would have danced itself into mayhem. Nothing that looked so normal now would exist this way tomorrow. That lady, for example, walking her dogs, throwing a stick for them on the playing field – what would she be doing tomorrow? Dancing? Lying down? Crashed out and helpless?

'Wait a minute!' he said. 'What about dogs?'

'Dogs?'

'Yes! Dogs! Of course. Dogs love humans.'

'So?'

'So, they'd listen to you and me, wouldn't they?'

'You bet,' Edie said.

'If we told them that the humans are going to be attacked by weird spiders, and only the dogs could save them, they'd help, wouldn't they?'

'Dogs aren't always the cleverest creatures,' Edie said, thoughtfully. 'But they aren't fools. They'd do what they could. Hopefully.'

'Who would win in a fight, a dog or one of your spiders?'

'Oh, a dog, easily! The spiders can only give very small nips.'

'Would their venom hurt the dogs?'

'I don't know. But if the dogs all did a lot

of dancing,' Edie said, smiling, 'and then they fell asleep, and then woke up feeling peaceful, would anyone notice?'

'Probably not,' Aubrey agreed. 'So that's what we have to do. Get all the spiders together, and get all the dogs together, and...'

'Your dogs against my spiders,' Edie exclaimed. 'Where? Back at the barn? I can get my spiders back there. But as soon as it gets dark they'll come pouring down the hill heading for the town. Anyone they find is going to get bitten. They're going to come right past your house – through your house, in fact.'

'Rushing Wood is the place,' Aubrey decided. 'It gives us the best chance of stopping them before they reach town.'

'OK,' said Edie. 'There's my mum now. I'll send out the code as soon as I get her phone. That will bring all the spiders back to the barn.'

'Will you help me with the dogs?'

Edie had a mischievous glint in her eye.

'Help you defeat my brilliant spiders?' she said. 'Don't the animals call you Aubrey Rambunctious Wolf? Let's see what you can do.'

CHAPTER 13

The Voice of the Woods and the Wild

When the story of the Battle of Rushing Wood is told – and it is told often, by animals, insects, birds, parents and children – one thing they all agree on is the role played by Lupo, the husky pup. Aubrey and Lupo were close friends. Aubrey told the pup his thoughts and stories, and the pup listened, and loved Aubrey, and tried to copy him in all he did.

When Aubrey got up in the morning feeling bouncy, Lupo bounced. When Aubrey sat down to do his homework, Lupo sat on his feet. If Aubrey watched a film or read a book on the sofa, Lupo tried to sit on him, and wished that he could read and follow the stories too.

Now, as the summer afternoon cast its gentle light over Rushing Wood, Aubrey met Villi the hornet, Ariadne the spider, Silvio the silverfish and Hoppy the squirrel behind the pond, where the bushes and briars made a sweet wild tangle, and the fence sagged, and the roots of the trees of Rushing Wood felt their way into the garden.

Hoppy had come down from a beech tree to sit on her favourite post. She teased Aubrey about how tall the boy was growing. 'I'll be able to build a drey in your hair soon!' she chittered. She teased Silvio about being out of the house in daylight (silverfish like to stay indoors, normally, as near to food as possible) and she teased Ariadne about her size: 'You're big for a spider but you don't scare me!'

Hoppy was teasing Villi about her battle with Aubrey when the squirrel saw Lupo the husky pup coming up the garden. She scolded and scrabbled, jumping into the hazel bush.

'There's that pup!' Hoppy chattered. 'That's the one that always chases me! Why did humans have to invent dogs? They chase anything! And most of them can't catch their own tails. Send it away, Aubrey! We can't discuss beating the Terrible Spiders with that thing hanging about.'

Lupo looked forlorn and left out. He put his head on one side and looked at Aubrey and whined, wagging his tail to show that he would be as obedient as possible, but really, couldn't he stay?

It is a strange fact that because dogs have lived so long with humans, and learned our ways so well, they have developed their own language of barks and whines and whimpers and pants, a language of wagging and licking and rolling and sitting, a language of jumping up and growling and lying down and sniffing, which enables them to communicate perfectly with us without using words. But in doing this they have lost the language of the wild.

Wild animals can talk to each other easily; they understand one another's calls and cries. But they understand dogs, and dogs understand them, only in the way that humans and dogs understand each other.

Your dog can bark at a fox or a hedgehog, but it cannot understand what they say. (This is probably a good thing, as what foxes and hedgehogs have to say about dogs is rarely polite.)

Only other dogs – and cats, of course; cats understand everything – can really understand the more subtle points of what a dog is trying to say.

'We have invited Lupo for a reason,' said Silvio, from his usual perch on Aubrey's shoulder: 'Lupo is a crucial part of the plan.'

'There's a plan?' squeaked Hoppy. 'Ha ha! All the woodland creatures are getting ready to watch thousands of Big B's spiders come cascading down the hill on their way to bite all the humans, but luckily, a silverfish has a plan!'

'And a hornet,' said Villi.

'And a spider,' said Ariadne.

Aubrey kept quiet. He felt it was not a human's place to make the decisions. If the men, women and children in the valley were to be saved from the Terrible Spiders, the creatures were going to have to save them.

'Let's hear it,' Hoppy said. 'Come on! Hit me! I bet this is going to be extremely funny. Three insects have a plan, it involves a husky pup, and Aubrey Rambunctious Wolf is part of it, but he's keeping very quiet. What's up, Bree?'

'I think Ariadne should say it,' Aubrey said. 'It's not up to humans anymore.'

'Well THAT makes a nice change!' Hoppy hollered. 'OK! Shoot!'

Ariadne waited for Hoppy to quieten.

'I've talked to the other spiders. We're going to help the humans. We don't want to see them get bitten and go loopy.'

'That's going to be a lot of help!' Hoppy squealed, delighted. 'Imagine that! A bunch of humans running away from a bunch of

Terrible Spiders, but it's OK, because real spiders, which they're terrified of, are going to help them! Ha ha! Hilarious! Have they got the silverfish on their side too?'

'Of course they have,' said Silvio, with dignity. 'We need humans. We regard them as good cooks, making meals for us.'

'Oh, well then, you can't lose!' Hoppy said to Aubrey, shaking with giggles. 'You've got the mighty silverfish. Look out, Terrible Spiders! The crumb-rollers are going to roll crumbs at you! Hee hee! And the hornets?'

'We are neutral,' said Villi, 'but we believe humans will blame us and the wasps for everything, so for our own sake we are going to help the humans too.'

'And sting the Terrible Spiders?' Hoppy yipped. 'Oh please say you are! That I have to see!'

'I have done the tactics and strategy,' Villi said. 'That's where Lupo comes in. Lupo is

going to get all the dogs in the valley to help
– if you agree?'

'If I agree?' Hoppy repeated, in astonish-
ment. 'What's it got to do with me? I just
want to watch!'

'We know that the dogs have not always
been kind to the wild creatures,' Aubrey
said.

'Right! Dogs are savages! They're killers!
They chase everything and the humans
don't stop them.'

'If the humans promise to stop the dogs
chasing the creatures of Rushing Wood,
will the creatures of Rushing Wood support
the dogs against the Terrible Spiders?'

Hoppy sat for a while. She looked very
surprised and thoughtful.

'You're serious? You need the animals so
much that you are going to change the way
humans behave, just like that? How?'

'When the humans learn that the dogs
and the wild creatures saved them from the

Terrible Spiders,' Aubrey said, 'they will try much harder for you. Look at the Great Animal Rebellion. Hardly anyone in the valley eats meat anymore. The humans are terrified, deep down. They are dead scared that everything is turning against them – the planet, the animals, even the weather is turning against them. The adults are beginning to understand that their own children are turning against them. They just need one chance to change, and this is it.'

Hoppy widened her huge bright eyes. She flicked her magnificent tail.

'One chance,' she said. 'I'd give it to you, Aubrey, because I love you. We grew up together, you in the house and me in these trees, and we're brother and sister really. All the animals like you. But we're called wild animals for a reason. We have the freedom of the wind in us, the freedom of the flying clouds. We grow up with the secrets of the mist and mysteries of the dark nights. We belong to the weather and the silence, to the moon, to storms, to daybreaks no human ever sees. We think for ourselves, act for ourselves, and many of us have no reason to love humans or dogs. All I can say is that each animal will make its own decision. Every creature must decide for itself if it would rather have a world of robots or a world of humans. That is all the help I can give you. Do you think it is less than humans deserve?'

Aubrey loved Hoppy. He stretched out his hand and the squirrel gave the end of his finger the lightest touch with her nose.

'One chance is all we ask,' he said.

Now Lupo barked and wagged his tail and Aubrey turned to him and smiled.

'Lupo!' he said. 'Run to Lola, to Little Frieda, to Lark and Apollo and Gyp. Tell them to tell Fly and Winston, Lulu and

Jess and Floss, and they must tell Frank and Benjy and Zappa – tell all the dogs, the humans need you. Tell them if they love us to come to Rushing Wood. The Terrible Spiders are coming for us, and only the dogs can stop them.'

With a small growl of determination and yip of glee at the importance of his mission, Lupo went. He was back in less than an hour, in time for his supper. He jumped up and wagged his tail at Aubrey.

Aubrey could not be entirely sure but he thought Lupo might just be saying, 'Done it!'

As the sun began to tilt behind the pine tree at the end of the valley where Ardea the heron sometimes perched, and the shadows lengthened and joined, and the last sunlight climbed slowly up the side of the valley, and blue shadows filled the meadow by the beck, the Terrible Spiders began to emerge.

They moved carefully at first, picking their way through the nettles, climbing over old stone walls, skittling under the bars of gates.

If you had been watching from the top of the barn, as a certain tawny owl was watching, your eye would have been caught, as his was, first by a movement, then another: the tawny owl's head spun this way and that as he spotted spider after spider twitching and scuttling, winding and jinking out of the barns and sheds.

The owl let out a loud 'Keey-whick!' which carried across the valley. Immediately owls in the trees below and the woods above took up his cry and passed it on. In a few moments, the call had been passed all the way from wood to wood for miles around. And in every wood, every creature heard the owls' cries, and all of them, now, knew what it meant.

The Terrible Spiders were coming.

Far down the slope below Rushing Wood, where the cottages of Woodside Terrace overlooked the meadow, Aubrey heard the owls. Lupo, whose ears were pointed and always alert, heard them too. He put his head on one side and growled.

'It's only owls, Lupo!' said Suzanne, scratching the little dog's head.

'They're early tonight,' said Jim. 'It's not even dark.'

'They do sometimes call in the twilight,' Suzanne said. 'I love it.'

'What are you up to, Aubrey Boy?' Jim asked. He could see his son was restless.

'Might take Lupo out for a little walk,' Aubrey said.

Aubrey was painfully undecided. Should he tell Jim and Suzanne to go up to the attic, shut the door and not come down until it was all over?

He knew they would never agree – if they were in danger, they would think that he must be in danger, and they would want to help him. If he told them the whole story, they would probably call the police. If that happened, Edie would be in trouble.

No, the best thing would be to make sure

they were not in danger by defending them, by winning the battle. If things went badly, he could always run back and warn them, and go to the attic with them if the spider tide could not be stopped.

He knew spider bites would not make him dance, not with all the wasp stings he had had, but he did not fancy being nipped and bitten.

The boy had faced fear before. He knew the way it grabs at your insides and makes the muscles of your legs feel cold and floppy. He knew how fear makes your body feel small and your voice squeaky, how it makes you want to run and hide. But he knew, too, that fear is a trick. Nothing is ever as frightening as it seems when you get to grips with it.

Every step you take towards the thing that frightens you makes you bigger and the fear smaller, he told himself.

He knew that fear could be overcome with courage, and he knew that courage comes from love. Like all children, Aubrey was full of love. He loved his family, his friends, the animals and the valley he lived in. He could not measure his love: it felt as wide as the universe. Compared to all the love his heart held, his fear was a small cold thing.

As he slipped out that night, with Lupo beside him, Aubrey told himself that love was stronger than fear, and that whatever happened in the battle he would do his very best. He took a good stick, and the rolling pin from the kitchen, because it made a solid club, and he tucked his trousers into his boots. But would it be enough?

The worst thing that could happen, he thought, was that he was about to get bitten a lot. He had a horrible vision of himself overwhelmed by a tide of biting robot spiders. It made him feel sick to imagine it. He tried to push the thought out of his mind. He took three deep breaths at the top of the garden, smelling the sweet scents of the evening, and breathed out, long and slowly, which made him feel calmer. Lupo the Bin Dingo was with him and Lupo seemed to sense his friend's fear. He whined, wagged his tail and prodded Aubrey's leg with his nose.

'Ready, Lupo? Did you tell the dogs?'

Lupo gave a small bark.

'Come on then,' said Aubrey. 'Let's face these spiders and finish them, once and for all.'

CHAPTER 14

The Battle of Rushing Wood

At first the woods were very quiet, as though they were listening to the padding paws of the husky pup and the footsteps of the boy. Few birds sang. A blackbird gave an alarm call and flashed into a bush. Aubrey walked quietly towards Frieda's Field.

A movement in the undergrowth above him made him spin round.

'Oh!' he gasped.

A huge dog was standing there. It was a great Irish wolfhound, shaggy and grey and as noble as a lion. Wolfhounds earned their name hundreds of years ago when they were bred to hunt deer and wolves and boars.

Aubrey smiled uncertainly. 'Hello,' he

said, but the dog looked so mighty and so dignified he added, 'Good evening!'

The wolfhound looked at him, steadily. Lupo, Aubrey noticed, had rolled on his back, put his paws in the air, and was giving the wolfhound his most beguiling look.

'You've come to help!' Aubrey whispered, hardly daring to believe it.

The dog seemed to inspect him for a few more moments, then the great shaggy tail twitched slightly, in what might have been something like the beginning of a wag. Now the wolfhound raised his head and barked three times. 'Roarw! Roarw! Roarw!'

Immediately the call was answered. There was a bark from somewhere nearby, and another, and another, and there came a rushing and crackling of paws flying through the wood, and now, to Aubrey's amazement, hundreds of shapes came pouring through the trees.

There were collies, Alsatians, Labradors,

poodles, otter hounds, terriers, malamutes, bulldogs, Bedlingtons, mastiffs, Great Danes, boxers, pointers, setters, Dobermans, dachshunds, Newfoundlands, springers and Airedales. There were labradoodles and cockapoos. There were lurchers and greyhounds. There were dozens of dogs with no breed names, dogs whose family stories went back hundreds of years and were full of adventures.

The astonishing thing was how quiet they were. Apart from those three answering calls, the dogs came dashing through Rushing Wood without barking or yapping or scrapping with each other. They were all excited, Aubrey could tell, but they were intent. They kept to some rule of silence of their own. When they saw the great wolfhound they stopped. Some sat. Some stood and sniffed the air. They all halted, and waited.

Aubrey hardly dared breathe. He had never

seen anything like it. Silvio poked his tiny head out of Aubrey's pocket.

'Woah,' he whispered. 'They've formed a pack – a megapack!'

Aubrey could only nod.

The wolfhound looked at Aubrey.

'I think he wants you to lead,' Silvio hissed.

'I can't! It should be him. I'm only small. Look at him!'

'You must,' Silvio whispered. 'If you want them to help then you must lead the way.'

Aubrey couldn't help raising his eyebrows in amazement and looking down at his friend.

'It's lucky you've watched so many films, or I wouldn't think this was the moment to take advice from a silverfish.'

'Go ON!' Silvio insisted.

Aubrey did it.

He nodded – in fact he almost bowed – to

the great wolfhound, and set off, feeling hundreds of dogs watching his every step. Sometimes just walking calmly is the bravest thing you can do.

So, calmly, Aubrey walked along the edge of the wood, took the path that led to Frieda's Field, opened the gate wide, and kept going, out across the grass.

Behind him he could hear hundreds of paws, padding.

A shape appeared beside him. It was the wolfhound. With Lupo on his left and the wolfhound on his right, he crossed the field. Neither dog looked back. Aubrey could hear the paws and pants behind him. For some reason he felt he should not look back either. Hundreds of dogs moving quietly together with such determination was extraordinary. It was something like a spell. Aubrey feared to break it.

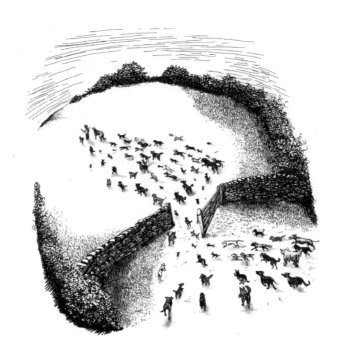

Lupo stopped first – his pointed ears were
the keenest in the valley. A tiny growl
began in the back of his throat. Now the
wolfhound paused, Aubrey stood still and
behind him every dog waited. The bushes on
the edge of the field above the steep bank of
the stream twitched and rustled.

And now the spiders came.

They came in a tide, like a slick of legs and

eyes and scuttling, hundreds of them oozing up over the bank. In an instant Aubrey realised what had happened. The spiders had crossed the fallen tree, a multitude of them, and now they were spreading out up and over the lip of the bank.

'We can stop them!' he cried. 'Now! Now we go!' And even as he realised what he had to do he was doing it.

Aubrey lifted his stick and his rolling pin and charged.

At once the wolfhound sprang forward. Even as Aubrey charged the nearest spiders the dogs came pouring past him. They reached the first of the terrible things and fell on the robots in a furious rush of snapping and biting.

Robot spiders were thrown in the air and savaged. How ferociously the dogs bit and chewed! It was as though every toy they had not been allowed to bite, every bone they had ever gnawed, every stick they had ever tugged and worried, every animal they had not been allowed to chase was alive and coming at them. It drove the dogs to a frenzy.

The spiders attacked, nipping and dashing, scrabbling and scuttling, and the dogs tore into them. Bigger dogs used their paws to crush them. Smaller dogs darted in and out, snapping and striking. White teeth flashed and slashed. The noise of the battle was savage barking and growling, snarling and cracking, shattering and crunching.

Where the fighting was thickest, Aubrey struck out again and again, bashing the machines into the earth, bursting and breaking them, battering and blasting them with clubbing blows. The dogs drove the machines back over the brink of the bank. Now they were hunting them on the slopes. Snarl and bite, dash and dodge, the bushes rocked and reeled and shook with the fighting.

If you have seen dogs fighting you will know how swiftly and fiercely a soppy, loving pet can defend itself.

For example, Lupo the Bin Dingo, the husky pup, seemed the sweetest creature, with his ears back, his eye looking huge and his tail wagging. But Lupo in the midst of a fight was a very different creature. All his hackles and his hair stood on end. He snarled in a savage way as he seized a spider in his jaws, lifted it and shook it violently, so fast and angrily the spider's legs flew off. With a crunch of his jaws Lupo drove his teeth deep into the spider's electronic guts and then flung it away with a toss of his head. With a bark of triumph he pounced on the next enemy.

From the top of the bank Aubrey could see down to the stream. The spiders were coming across the fallen tree in a column. But the column was only two or three spiders wide.

'Of course!' he cried. 'They're electric! They can't swim – they can't cross water. If we can get to the fallen tree, we can beat them there. Ow!'

A spider bit him on the ankle.

Lupo rushed in and crunched it.

'Thanks, Lupo. Look out!' Aubrey cried, and struck behind the pup, at another spider, and again, at another. The great wolfhound appeared with a lurcher and a collie beside him. Together they worked, slaying and smashing the robot spiders in a flurry of snarls and snaps.

'Great fighting!' shouted Silvio.

'Come, Lupo!' Aubrey cried. 'Charge! We can win it!'

Down the bank went the boy and the dogs together. Occasionally a dog would growl as it found a spider, and then would come another burst of snarls and a crackling of parts.

Aubrey was beating the terrible machines back down the bank with mighty swings of his clubs. He could see the battle was being won, but fighting is dreadfully hard work: he and all the dogs were panting, and his arms were beginning to tire.

'We can do it!' he shouted, and the dogs rallied again, driving their enemy down and back towards the water.

The Terrible Spiders did not react like living beings might. They did not panic or turn or run; they had to be beaten, crushed, crunched and broken, every single one of them. Any that were missed kept coming, kept attacking, with robot determination. The dogs hunted them up the bank and along the edge of the field.

With a last ferocious effort Aubrey made it to the end of the fallen tree. Now the battle was easier – only three spiders at a time.

Most of the spiders that had crossed had been destroyed, but there were more on the other side. Still they came.

Now there was a hoot from the branches above them. It was a tawny owl.

'There are more!' cried the owl. 'More, more!'

'Where?'

'Coming down the fields.'

'Come on, dogs!'

They beat the last of the spiders crossing the fallen tree and climbed back up the bank. Aubrey was shattered.

The wolfhound ran up to Aubrey and licked his hand, just once. He bounded off across the field, followed by all the dogs, from the largest Great Dane to the smallest terrier.

'Where are they going?'

'Home to their masters and mistresses, home to their children, home to their suppers and beds,' said the owl, flying low over the boy and landing on an anthill.

'And there are more Terrible Spiders coming?'

'They are coming down the track out of the wood. They crossed the stream higher up.'

The boy looked up.

There they were.

Pouring down the high track from the wood into the field came the second prong of the spiders' attack. They looked, Aubrey thought, like a kind of oil slick – shining and glittering, rushing down towards him, covering the field in clicking darkness. He suddenly felt exhausted. Without the dogs the battle was lost.

'We're beaten,' he panted. 'It's the end.'

'Not necessarily,' said the owl. 'What is the first rule of the countryside?'

'Um – always shut the gate?'

'Correct. And you didn't! Look behind you.'

CHAPTER 15
Humans Are Animals Too

M r Greenwood's cows had been enjoying their new freedom since their farmer took up gardening and growing vegetables. Now that they had lost their fear of humans, they found the world a very different place. Leaning hard on a gate that was only tied shut with string, they found, would open it. Butting a fence post hard would topple it. If any human tried to chase them about, swinging their heads at him or her and mooing would soon change that human's mind.

And so the cows went where they wanted and did what they wished to do, which was mostly mooching about and eating grass. The trails of open gates and flattened fences they left behind them were a treat for other farm animals. Horses wandered the lanes. Three llamas haunted the woods. Sheep went adventuring over the moors. Pigs rootled in the undergrowth. Goats climbed among the crags.

In this way the farm animals had mingled with the creatures of Rushing Wood. When news came of the Night of the Terrible Spiders, none of the animals liked the sound of it. What were these things, they asked each other, what were these creature-machines which had come pouring out of Hollins Hall, set on biting and terrorising the town?

Perhaps the animals would have left it at that – it was hard to know what to think, after all, about humans and their strange ways – if the word had not gone out among them that Edie, otherwise known as Big B, wanted their help. The farm animals cared for Edie as much as the wild ones were fond of Aubrey. Edie's magnificent black mare, Thunder, had told all the farm animals what a loving and considerate girl her Edie was. And it was Thunder, the great black mare, who Aubrey saw first when he turned and looked at the gate he had forgotten to close.

Thunder was thundering into the field, and there was Edie, riding her! Galloping and cantering and trotting and dashing after her were horses and llamas, pigs and goats, a great white bull and a stampede of heifers and bullocks.

Edie swung her horse away from the galloping animals and brought Thunder to a plunging stop beside her friend.

'Need some help, Aubrey Rambunctious Wolf?'

Aubrey shouted with delight and relief.

'Oh, yes please!'

'Come up then,' she said, and helped Aubrey climb up onto Thunder's back behind her.

'Go, Thunder! Go, beautiful! Charge!' Edie cried, and they swept up the field at a gallop.

Soon they were among the Terrible
Spiders. The animals trampled and
crushed the machines, pounding and
pulverising, squashing and raking them.
The bullocks loved it, running hither and
thither, jumping and jolting, stamping
and snorting. The horses whinnied as they
reared and stamped. When they reached
the last knot of the Terrible Spiders Aubrey
dismounted and fought on foot. Edie turned
Thunder to charge and charge again.

A gang of the robots rushed at Aubrey and
brought him to his knees. He laid about
him with stick and rolling pin in a flurry of
blows, driving the spiders off, beating them
back and thumping them into the ground.
Two goats sprang up to help him, and
Lupo was still beside him, faithful as ever,
protecting his master as best he could.

Edie and Thunder circled back. Edie
reached down and helped Aubrey scramble

up behind her. Aubrey was too exhausted to speak. It was all he could do to hang on to Edie and gasp as he got his breath back.

When the last of the Terrible Spiders had been smashed, the animals stood panting, nuzzling each other and picking over the grazing.

Edie jumped down from Thunder. Aubrey climbed down slowly, carefully. Ariadne appeared on his shoulder.

The light was almost gone now. The moon rose, casting a white-blue glow over the valley. The animals began to drift away, following their noses to the best grass, the cattle trooping quietly up the path towards the wood. The stars came out, like lanterns over the wood. Edie patted Thunder's nose and told her she was the mightiest horse in the world.

Aubrey sat down on the grass.

'If you hadn't come to help,' he said, 'I couldn't have stopped them.'

'I was watching,' Edie replied. 'We could only stop them together.'

For a while the children said nothing. They stared up at the peaceful moon.

'The adults won't even know we've saved them,' Edie said, after a while.

'I wish they'd seen the battle,' Aubrey said. 'I wish they knew the whole story.'

'We know, at least,' said Edie. 'And all the animals and the wild creatures know.'

Lupo whined and wagged his tail. 'And the dogs know best of all!' Aubrey laughed.

Edie reached down a hand and pulled him up to his feet.

'You are a great leader,' he told her. 'You can do anything!'

'And you are a true warrior for peace,' Edie said. 'You saved the town, and the people.'

'And you were the greatest of all,' Aubrey said to Thunder, Lupo and Silvio. 'Without the animals the humans were lost.'

He patted the horse and stroked the dog. He felt their warmth through his hands.

'Humans are animals too,' said Silvio, climbing up on to Aubrey's other shoulder, from where he had been sheltering from the fight in a pocket.

'You just need to remember it!' Ariadne added. She winked at Aubrey and Edie with some of her many eyes.

The children and the animals laughed, and they all walked together, out of the field and back to their homes, to their lives, their families and their friends, to their passions and their plans.

That was not quite the end of the story.

Perhaps it was not just Aubrey and Edie who could speak with animals. Perhaps one of the dogs took their humans to see the battlefield. Or perhaps there was someone watching over the wall, a walker or a runner, when the battle of Rushing Wood was fought on Frieda's Field.

In the days that followed some mysterious vans appeared in the lane, and men and women who did not say much put tape on the gate and collected all the thousands of bits of broken spiders and took them away for 'analysis'. Nothing was ever heard about them again. No questions were asked.

But something changed in the valley. Perhaps it had to do with that mixture of sheep hormones and potions Edie had concocted to make people love like ewes and dance like lambs. Farm animals were allowed to wander at will through the lanes and over the moors and fields, which put an end to the Great Animal Rebellion.

Someone had the idea of putting up a sign at the entrance to the town which said,

'This Town Is Animal-Friendly!' The animals could not read, but they noticed a change in the way humans treated them. Even the insects noticed it, when people stopped splatting then and the farmers stopped using pesticides, and soon there were many more of them – insects, I mean. And a few more farmers, too.

Many more birds were seen, and there were more wild creatures in the woods. A new spirit came over the valley, something simple and joyful and good. You could feel it in the days, and hear it in the birdsong. You could almost see it when the skies were bright. You could catch the joy of this spirit in the bustle of dogs taking their owners for walks, in the tiny fireworks of flowers in the hedges and the happy yells of children playing.

Adults and visitors to the town were often slightly mystified by this spirit. It was all around but hard to grasp, like trying to catch falling leaves. 'I don't know what it is,' someone or other would say, 'but it feels lovely!'

Whenever they heard this, the birds (especially Corone and the jackdaws), the insects (especially Villi, the magnificent hornet, and the brave wasps Vizzy and Zivvy, and their cunning Guard Captain), and the wild animals (including Hoppy, of course), and the farm animals like Barbara the black hen, and Thunder the horse, and dogs like Lupo, and our heroes, Silvio and Ariadne and Edie and Aubrey, and children like you all knew exactly what it was, and they grinned.

It is the spirit that lives inside us all.
It is the opposite of war.
It is the secret of life. It is the soul of love.
And the name of this spirit is
Friendship!

Praise for
Aubrey and the Terrible Yoot
(winner, Branford Boase Award 2015)

'Horatio Clare writes about animals
as well as T. H. White.'

'...something very special – a book that is
both pensive and sparkling with originality
and life. It is a testament to the healing
power of the imagination.'

'A beautiful and touching story, told
in a unique and refreshingly original style.'
' ... it shines a light on mental health
without ever feeling like a manual'

Branford Boase judges

'Here is writing and storytelling at its best. Here is a wondrous tale, from a writer who loves language ... a book of ideas, full of learning, though you might not know it, because you are enjoying it so much. Here is a tale that sweeps you along inside its magic, and its hope. At once bubbling with joy, and at the same time dealing with the great sadness that overcomes so many of us in our lives, the Terrible Yoot of the title. A daring book, beautifully conceived, and supremely well written. Horatio Clare has the voice of a great storyteller ... a joy, a sheer joy!

Michael Morpurgo

'What a treasure ... rambunctious spirit, massive heart, and a poet's eye. It's also really funny.'

Frank Cottrell Boyce

'A poetic and profound story ... with captivating drawings by Jane Matthews, it's a magical wintery adventure told with a unique mix of robust humour and imaginative insight. Highly recommended for children aged eight-plus.'

Amanda Craig, New Statesman's best children's books of 2015

'A jewel not to be missed is Horatio Clare's debut children's book Aubrey and the Terrible Yoot ... about a rambunctious boy's quest, helped by talking woodland animals, to break the spell of despair that has overwhelmed his father. This is a funny, big-hearted, nimble, original story, with a quality of fairy tale, informative footnotes, a sensitive way of dealing with the important subject of depression and engaging black- and-white illustrations by Jane Matthews.'

Nicolette Jones, children's books of the year, Sunday Times

'A heartening reminder that while the world may be puzzling and fraught it is also full of beauty and magic.'

The Independent

'This is a completely wonderful insight into depression, I wish this book had been around to help someone I know. Poignant, funny, unique and ultimately uplifting, don't miss this gem.'

Lara Mieduniecki, Blackwell's, Edinburgh

'This remarkable novel is full of lyrical writing and sensible thinking...'

Gwales.com

' ...an imaginative and thoughtful adventure ... the story is as lighthearted as it is serious. Beautifully illustrated by Jane Matthews, both young and old will enjoy this book.'

We Love This Book

'This is a special and unusual book ...
some beautiful writing conjures up the
sights, sounds and smells of the countryside
with such clarity that you'll feel the damp
ground beneath your feet, but it's also a
moving and thoughtful description of a
young boy trying to help his father through
depression... a story full of
tenderness and understanding.'

Lovereading4kids

'This clever book mixes myth, fable and
modern family life to create a vivid story
that is not only full of magic but also looks
sympathetically at complex issues such as
depression. The story does not shy away
from this difficult topic, but describes
it in a gentle and age-appropriate way,
engendering understanding rather than
fear. This is an enjoyable book that deals
with important issues not often covered in
writing for this age range.'

Books for Keeps Book of the Week

'Over the years I've met and read ... a host of great writers who can engage and transport children. Today I heard Horatio Clare introduce and launch Aubrey and The Terrible Yoot. It's about a rambunctious boy who needs to save his father. There was a small roomful of children who had their capacity for wonder and adventure met with humour and imagination and humanity of the most delightful kind. There was also the sense that we were the first people to meet this book, and that that in itself was a privilege and something we all might get to tell our grandchildren about. We were there.'

Peter Florence

'...an enjoyable, intriguing and important book.'

Armadillo Magazine

CHAPTER 1

Rambunctious Boy

Aubrey's first scream was so loud it blew the wax out of his nurse's ears. All babies cry when they are born, but Aubrey's WAAAWWLL! was so fierce it also set off a doctor's car alarm.

She was an elderly nurse with a face like a kindly gargoyle. She washed him and wrapped him in a blanket.

'This child has the howl of a wolf!' the nurse exclaimed.

Aubrey took another breath and yowled so loudly he went purple. He kicked like mad too, catching the nurse a good hoof in the guts as she handed him to his mother.

'Guh!' she gasped. 'And he's...' she searched for the right word, unable to breathe until she found it, '...Rambunctious!'

The nurse could not remember the last

time she had said 'rambunctious' but she knew that it was an American word which means exactly what it sounds like. Blowing out ear wax, winding his midwife and setting off a car alarm were Aubrey's first rambunctious acts, and he achieved them in under a minute.

There is a theory that very small children subconsciously remember everything they hear. I don't know if it's true, but *Rambunctious! Wolf!* It might explain what happened next.

Next, when he was less than a year old, Aubrey saw someone running past the house where he lived with his parents. He decided it was time he ran, too. At his age wolf cubs can run marathons. Aubrey had barely learned how to stand.

Quick! he thought, get moving!

He jumped up, threw himself forward and flung out a leg, just like the runner. His body kept going forward but the leg gave up suddenly. The floor flipped up and bashed him. He tried again, many times...

Bonk, bump, thump

...it was like listening to apples rolling off a table.

'That's Aubrey again, smashing the place up,' remarked Mr Ferraby with a grin, as the thuds and blows of Aubrey's running practice reverberated through Woodside Terrace. The Ferrabys lived next door. Mr Ferraby was an expert on the astonishing array of sounds Aubrey created as he became bigger, stronger and more adventurous.

Aubrey's parents begged him to be patient.

'Please try walking first!' implored his mother, Suzanne. Suzanne was a nurse. She knew her son was tough but she was worried he would hurt himself.

'It's the traditional next step!' his father said. Jim was an English teacher who loved stories. He was secretly delighted that his son did not seem interested in following the normal story pattern of stand, then walk, then run.

The little boy ignored them both. He specialised in ignoring Jim and Suzanne. He loved them, but you can't spend too much time listening to your parents, not if you want to live to the limit.

'Live To The Limit' was Aubrey's philosophy at this point. Having a philosophy is a very good thing, especially if it leads you on a life-saving quest.

However, having a philosophy is not such a good thing if it leads you to crash two cars before you are old enough to drive one, which was Aubrey's next trick.

When he was four years old Aubrey thought it might be fun to take the car for a spin. He had often watched his parents driving: it was easy. One Sunday afternoon, when his father was upstairs sleeping

FOOTNOTE: Aubrey's philosophy at this point is somewhere near Hedonism: live life for pleasure and excitement, nothing is more important. An ancient Greek genius called Democritus came up with the idea that contentment and happiness are the aim of a well-lived life, and if you feel them, it proves you are living well. You might feel it does not take a genius to come up with that but Democritus also came up with the idea of atoms, two thousand years before their existence was proved.
FOOTNOTE TO FOOTNOTE: Like Hedonism, atoms turn out to be something of a mixed blessing.

under one of his favourite books, and his mother was in the garden, poking around in the vegetable patch and talking to the woodpigeons, Aubrey climbed a chair and took the car key off the table. He was banned from using the front door by himself because the lane was just there, but now he did – using the chair again to reach the catch – and stepped out. He pointed the key at the car and pressed the button. The car clicked and flashed its lights at him in a friendly way.

'Hello car!' Aubrey whispered.

The view from the driving seat was mostly sky, with a steering wheel across it. He stood up on the seat: much better! He could see down the lane towards town, and he could see Rushing Wood rising up on both sides of the valley, and he could see Mr and Mrs Ferraby's smart blue German car, parked smack in front of him. He would have to go around that.

Although Aubrey forgot to put the key in

the ignition, which meant that the engine did not switch on, which meant he was never going to get very far, he did not forget to let the handbrake off. He had watched Jim and Suzanne haul it up, push the button and let it down. Aubrey did this with both hands while standing on the seat. It worked a treat. The lane just there tilts slightly down towards the town, so as soon he released the brake the car began to move.

'Yup!' cried Aubrey. It was one of his favourite words.

'YUP!' he shouted, as the car began to roll properly, and he turned the steering wheel hard to the right, because Mr and Mrs Ferraby's car was very close now and he had to go round it or –

CRUNCH!

Mr Ferraby's car began to shout and wail
like a goose and a donkey having a fight
- HONK HONK! - HEE HAAW! -
and flash all its lights in distress.

Because Woodside Terrace is a very quiet
place, where nothing really disturbs the
peace except the postman, the parking
ticket patrol, the waste disposal truck, the
delivery lorry to the tearoom in the old mill,
the 10,000 tourists who pass every summer
on their way to explore the Rushing Wood,
as well as all the people who go walking,
running, cycling and exercising dogs every
day, the sound of car alarms is seldom heard
there. Mr Ferraby had never even heard
his car's alarm before. He burst out of his
house, ready to rescue his beloved machine.
Thieves, bandits and vandals were rarely
seen on Woodside Terrace but now Mr
Ferraby imagined a horde of them attacking
Liebling Trudi. (This was his secret name
for his car, because she was so German, so
glossy and so sleek.)

FOOTNOTE: Liebling is German for
'Darling'.

Mr Ferraby believed he was going to have to fight about ten vandals and/or bandits, certainly two or three. He was determined to defend Liebling Trudi to the last. His chances of victory were non-existent, he knew, and it was a pity he must die now, in the prime of his late middle age, but if his time had come he was ready. His doomed last stand would make Trudi proud of him, and Mrs Ferraby too.

Braced for a death-struggle with all the crazy-faced cohorts of hell, Mr Ferraby was entirely unprepared for the sight of Aubrey, standing in the driving seat of his father's car – the nose of which was rammed into the back of Liebling Trudi – gripping the wheel with both hands and smiling a reassuring smile. 'You little vandal bandit!' Mr Ferraby cried.

to read more, look for *Aubrey and the Terrible Yoot* at your local bookshop or on our website
www.fireflypress.co.uk